SIMPLY GREGG

A DETECTIVE STORY

EVELYN INFANTE

Cover Design by Wesley Goulart

Publisher:

Shaggy Dog Productions
www.ShaggyDogProductions.online

"For the sins of your fathers you, though guiltless, must suffer."

— HORACE, ODES III, 6.1.1

PROLOGUE
LAST CASE

I t started innocently enough.

My wife and I were having my den painted the next morning. Days ago, Louise had asked me to get rid of the boxes filled with paperwork I used to occasionally take home to study during a homicide investigation. Now that I'm retired, she reasoned, I didn't need to keep these old files cluttering up my office.

My boxes had been stacked neatly in a corner of the room for years now, not bothering anyone, or so I thought. Louise did have a point though, so I promised to move the files to the garage for now and shred them all, once the paint dried.

When I raised the garage door, beams of sunshine sparkling with dust particles, streamed through the windows and momentarily captivated me. The natural light accentuated the many spider webs on the shelves, the sawdust on the work-table, and the many items jumbled and out of place. This was not going to be a two-minute job. I shook my head and took a deep breath. I'd been putting off this chore for far too long.

First things first. Leaving my boxes on the dolly, I opened a drawer, and took out a dust mask and a bandana. I put in my earbuds, chose an upbeat playlist, and got to work.

My stomach began to growl with hunger as the afternoon approached, despite the usual big breakfast Louise had prepared that morning. I chose to ignore the pangs of discomfort knowing I wouldn't finish today if I stopped for lunch.

By late afternoon, it was all coming together. The tools were hung neatly on the wall, shelves dusted, chemicals properly organized and new shelves put up to clear the floor. I had tossed out any empty containers I came across and moved all the small machinery including the lawn mower into its proper area. I even cleaned the windows which I had left wide open all morning to help clear out the musty air.

Finally, my muscles aching, I forced myself to sweep the floor and bring the garbage to the curb. Best of all, I'd cleared enough room to move the cars back into our double garage. That, above all else, would make my wife happy. She hated parking her car outdoors. She'd had incidents in the past when it had been damaged by falling tree branches or covered in muddy critter prints.

I was more than ready for a break by then. My sweaty shirt was sticking to my skin, my hands were filthy, and the bandana keeping the sweat out of my eyes, was soaked.

I hosed down my grimy hands at the garden spigot and splashed water on my neck and face, drying myself with paper towels. Back inside the garage, I grabbed a Heineken out of the mini fridge and sat at my workbench to wait for my wife, who was due home any minute from her volunteer job at the retirement apartments. I knew I should have been heading toward a long, hot shower, but I wanted to see her face when she saw what I'd done. Besides, after all that work, I needed to sit for a while. My muscles hadn't had a workout in a long time.

Where had the day gone? Only a couple of hours left till sundown. No wonder I was hungry.

I sat back and surveyed my work, feeling an enormous sense of accomplishment. That's when my eyes gazed at the boxes of case files I had temporarily stashed in the corner. Staring at the boxes as if I'd never seen them before, my mind began to drift back to my last homicide investigation.

I had fully intended to relax while I waited for Louise, but as I sipped the well-deserved lager and stared at the boxes, an uncontrollable desire took hold. Without another thought, I chugged the rest of my beer and got off the bench.

I scanned the labels until I found the one marked, 2003 CASES. I rummaged through the files and found the folders on the Romero homicide. What was it about that particular case? I couldn't tell you. All I knew for sure, was that something about that case still nagged at me. Perhaps it was simply a desire to re-experience my last days as a homicide detective.

I flipped open one of the Romero folders and found a few newspaper clippings.

I read one from a 2003 edition of the Pocono Record.

February 16, 2003 – East Stroudsburg. Mr. Felix Romero, Age 58, was savagely tortured and killed in his home last night while his wife, Elena, slept. Stroud Area Regional Police asks anyone with any information relevant to this crime to call the Anonymous Tip Line at (570) 424-7002, 24 hours/day. All calls will be kept confidential.

I SET the folder of newspaper clippings aside and opened another, diving into the case as I imagined the events of the night Felix Romero died.

I was still pouring over the records when Louise walked in with a smile, a dinner tray, and a kiss.

"Thank you, Howie. Love what you did with the place," she said, before leaving me with a plea not to stay up all night.

1

NOSTALGIA

It's been a little over two years since my retirement, and I still find myself yearning for action, not that leaving the job behind was hard. After all, three decades chasing the scum of the Earth does wear you down. All the same, I do miss the challenge. I even miss the dead ends and frustrations that go along with the job.

Most of all, I miss my team. We didn't just work well together—we were also a family. There's no feeling in the world like the camaraderie and cooperation I got whenever I was working a case with my guys. Between chasing clues, brainstorming, and putting the pieces together to solve a case, adrenaline flowed through my veins from start to finish. When we zeroed in on a suspect and took him down…yeah. That was the ultimate high.

On my last day before my retirement, I walked out of 100 Dey Street a man still loving the job after many decades, a little sad, a little tired, yet incredibly grateful for the career chosen so many years ago. Sure, I've witnessed my share of horrors over the years, but that's not what gave me a sour taste. Instead, it was the plea-bargaining, the court delays, and the damn defense lawyers. Those parts of the job I definitely do not miss.

Every once in a while I'd come across a newspaper article about a murder in the Poconos and without even thinking about it, I'd start questioning every detail and wondering how the team was doing with the investigation. A few times, I was even curious enough to call one or two of my former teammates and pump them for information, but it didn't take me long to realize I was being more of a bother than a help. No one wants a player who's left the game to quarterback from the sidelines, as they say.

I felt like an old racehorse who despite being put out to pasture, still yearns for the track. Louise saw that and kept me from breaking through the barn door. Once a cop, always a cop certainly rings true with me.

Unlike some law enforcement officers, who at the end of their careers have no one to share the rest of their lives with, I am fortunate enough to be married to a patient and understanding woman. After all those years putting up with the late hours and midnight phone calls, she deserves my full attention and gratitude. She and I have spent the last couple of years traveling and reconnecting after my retirement.

Louise and I had made sure to prioritize family time while the kids were growing up. Despite my hectic schedule, we even managed to squeeze in date nights every now and then. Things were difficult at times, but we made our marriage work.

It takes a special kind of woman, of course, to live that kind of life. Some, hell, most women who aren't in the field themselves, can't handle the stress of being married to a law enforcement officer. Divorce is prevalent among my colleagues. I'm one of the lucky ones. I got out unscathed. At least I think I did.

Wrapping up my last case before that final walk out of the precinct was the finishing touch to my thirty-three years on the job. All the more so because of how tricky the case had been —

jumping more than a few hurdles along the way. Yes, that one was a bitch to crack. Don't know how I could've retired if that homicide hadn't been solved on my watch.

But I tell you, some cases stay with you long after you've closed the books on them, like my last one.

2

FELIX

The Presidents' Day blizzard of 2003 was a monster, moving up the east coast of the United States and Canada. Some were even calling it the storm of the century. With snow falling at a rate of four inches per hour, and winds gusting between thirty and sixty miles per hour, whiteout conditions were widespread throughout the Poconos.

Felix Romero, who had lived in New York City most of his life, had never before lived through such a severe winter. If it snowed in New York, the city would quickly recover. Public transportation, schools, and businesses rarely closed on account of the weather.

In the Poconos, a few flakes fall, thought Felix sarcastically, and *everything shuts down*.

It was all his wife's fault as far as he was concerned. She was the one who had convinced him to blow their savings on this piece of shit house, in this godforsaken place, where it's been snowing since winter began.

A few moments ago, Elena had banished him from their comfortable king-sized bed, claiming his snoring "threatened to shake the very foundations of the house." Felix never used to snore. It only ever happened when he had been drinking heavily. Lately, he'd been doing that quite a lot.

Banished to the frigid guestroom, Felix knew he was in for an uncomfortable night. He couldn't even turn on the electric heat, a thing he almost never did unless forced to do so. "Why turn on the electric heat, no matter how low, to warm a room that is never in use?" he'd argued with Elena when they'd first moved in. He now wished he'd listened and kept the thermostat at least at its lowest setting.

Grumbling in annoyance, he lifted the lid from the storage bench at the foot of the bed, and pulled out two bedspreads, laying them on top of the already made bed. He then crawled under the covers and wrapped himself up like a mummy.

Shivering from his head to his woolen socks, he lay there, and listened as the raucous storm whipped the icy precipitation into a frenzy, with no regard for power lines, water pipes, or people nestled in their beds, in unheated rooms.

He was almost certain he could feel his poorly-built house vibrating from all four corners. He feared the weight of the snow accumulating on the roof would bring the house down on them at any moment.

Ever since he moved out of the city, insomnia had become a way of life for Felix. No matter what time he came to bed, he could never settle down unless he had drunk himself into a stupor. Elena had already been asleep by the time Felix stumbled into bed that night, drunk and miserable. He finally dozed off, only to be awakened soon after on account of his snoring, and ordered out of bed.

Cold and alone in the guestroom, he sighed, *I had to come to the Poconos.*

Yesterday, he'd almost lost his life getting to and from work, only to be stuck there for hours with barely anything to do.

Although grateful he wouldn't have to endure another day driving around the Poconos after a blizzard, he was worried.

He could not afford any time off with his paltry hourly wage. His wife, who hadn't worked since before their marriage, also brought in meager pay from her job washing hair at the local beauty salon. Felix, meanwhile, had gotten desperate enough to take a job meant for teenagers. He thought this beneath them.

It seemed only yesterday he was on top of the world. He had made good money as a senior lending officer for a bank on Wall Street, though he spent a lot of it hanging out with coworkers, bar hopping, and flirting.

Felix had been working at the bank since 1968, the same year he graduated college. His reward for his thirty-one years of service was twelve-months' severance and the door. Unemployed for the first time in his life, Felix was confident a man with his background would have no problem finding a job commensurate with his experience.

After nearly two years of pounding the pavement, Felix still hadn't managed to secure a job offer worth his consideration. More than one headhunter had tried to talk him into taking an entry-level job. They all said it was the best they could do for him. No way was Felix willing to start over from the bottom. The very idea was an insult to his ego. He began to suspect the industry prized younger people, whom they could pay a lot less, over senior-level executives like himself.

Felix was only fifty-eight, too young to retire, yet his pizza delivery job caused him great humiliation. It angered him to think the rich get richer while everyone else gets fucked. He was sick of it all.

How did I come to this? he asked himself for the hundredth time.

On this cold winter's night, white and uncaring, filled with the brutality and force of nature, an uneasy foreboding took hold of him.

Restless, he turned toward the undraped window. He could see nothing but darkness in the moonless night. As he stared, he felt the blackness seep into his very soul. Like the storm churning the atmosphere outside, a tempest of self-pity whipped Felix from within, filling his throat with despair, and making his eyes smart with tears.

Felix sat up hoping to shake off his gloomy mood. He took a few deep breaths to conquer the queasiness in his gut, cleared the lump in his throat, and wiped the tears from his eyes.

That's when his mind turned to his shitty day.

Felix had slept through his alarm that morning and hadn't had time to eat breakfast before dashing out of the house. Hungry and irritable, he stopped by the local bakery to pick something up on his way to work. He had been looking forward to his buttered onion bagel until the owner informed him she couldn't break his five.

"Why don't you buy something else, so I don't have to give you back so much change?" she'd suggested.

"Why are you even open if you're not prepared to serve your customers?" Felix snarled.

According to the proprietor, she'd opened the shop early that morning to make sure the plow drivers had somewhere they could get breakfast before heading out to clear the roads. She had meant to get to the bank yesterday, but the shop got busy, and she never got around to it. By the time the rush ended, the bank was already closed.

Felix wasn't having it. He went to the bakery regularly for her freshly-baked bagels, so he wasn't fooled by her fumbling explanations. He didn't believe for a second the owner of a very popular bake shop wouldn't have change for a measly five-dollar bill. Her excuses only fueled his anger.

"If you're not going to buy anything, leave or I'll call the police," she snapped back at him, eyes flashing.

Without thinking, Felix threw the bagel in her face and stormed out of the bakery. He could grab coffee at the pizzeria and didn't want to be forced into buying coffee or anything else from that damn woman.

Felix struggled through the wind to his car, which was already covered in snow. Cursing, he unlocked the door, turned on the ignition, switched on the heat to full blast, and reached for the snow brush. The snow was falling so thick and fast by then, the brush did little to clear the windshield.

Hands ice cold and numb, he got back into the car and switched on the wipers to their highest speed. He held his hands over the heat vents for a minute, vigorously rubbing them together to try to bring some feeling back. He was anxious as he contemplated the two miles from the bakery to the pizzeria. He put the car in drive and slowly pulled out onto the street.

He had only been on the road for a minute or two when he happened to glance at the gas gauge.

Damn it to hell!

Just under a quarter tank. If he was going to do deliveries in this weather, he had better fill up.

His empty stomach was growling repeatedly by the time he found an open gas station with only a couple of cars waiting their turn. Although the wait was only a few minutes, it felt much longer to the famished Felix. He would get something to eat in the mini mart after he filled up, he decided, as he put the nozzle in the gas tank.

Gas tank full, he returned the nozzle to its holder and waited for the machine to dispense his receipt. Nothing happened. He let out a choice string of expletives before storming into the mini mart.

"Someone should get off his lazy ass and put paper in the machine," he yelled at the startled cashier.

"Sorry, Sir. I didn't realize the dispenser was out of paper," he said with a cautious smile. "I can print a receipt for you now. May I have the pump number?"

Nerves frayed and stomach growling, Felix's instinct was to

wipe that pathetic smile off the idiot cashier's face. Instead, he stomped out of the mini mart without another word.

By the time he got to the pizzeria, he was ready to snap.

"Late again, Felix? I can't imagine what could have kept you today," laughed Mr. Conte, the owner of the shop, before Felix even had a chance to take off his coat and shake off the snow. "I made it in at my regular starting time. Why didn't you?"

The look Felix answered him with, made it clear he was in no mood for jokes.

"I'm only kidding. Glad to see you made it safely."

Tired, hungry, and pissed off, Felix could not see how his boss could joke about him being late. Of course, Mr. Conte had gotten here on time. He lives in the apartment above the pizzeria. For him to expect Felix to risk his life to get to a job he hated, was no joking matter, as far as Felix was concerned.

"I risk my life driving here in these conditions, and you think it's funny to *joke* about it?"

"All right, Felix. I apologize," said Mr. Conte.

Felix marched over to the coffee pot and poured himself a large cup without bothering to acknowledge the apology.

He had put a lot of effort into getting to work, for which he didn't feel at all appreciated.

Thankfully, not a single order came in that day. He felt almost certain he would have gotten into an accident if he needed to make a delivery. The storm didn't look like it would let up any time soon.

The morning dragged on as Felix cleaned, stacked boxes, and prepped ingredients. All the while under his breath, Felix cursed anyone and everyone he felt had wronged him that day —his boss, the bakery owner, the gas station attendant. He even cursed his wife for letting him sleep through the alarm, which is why he ended up rushing out of the house without breakfast.

Damn them.

The battery-operated radio on the counter confirmed many businesses had closed early due to power outages and unpassable roads. Elena had already called a couple of times begging Felix to come home.

"I can't go home until the shop closes, Elena. It's not like I have a choice."

Mr. Conte overheard the conversation and immediately regretted making Felix come in. He could have kicked himself for underestimating the weather.

"Felix, I've decided to close up early. Please drive carefully on your way home. Radio says the storm is getting stronger."

Although relieved to get out before the storm got any worse, Felix hadn't made any tips to supplement his hourly wage that day. He worried he wasn't going to be able to meet his expenses for the month.

Perhaps trying to make up for the morning's tactless joke, or possibly because he felt guilty for making Felix come in at all, Mr. Conte offered him the two pizza pies he had baked earlier.

"Please take these home with you, Felix. I'd rather your family eat them than to let them go to waste. See you Monday."

Embarrassed, Felix bowed his head and mumbled a thanks as he accepted the gift.

The charity exhibited by Mr. Conte only intensified Felix's sense of worthlessness. He wanted nothing more than to throw the pies in the garbage, but he couldn't afford to turn down a free meal.

The drive home, normally a quick twenty-minute trip, took Felix almost an hour that day. Creeping along at twenty miles per hour down the less-trafficked back roads, Felix had to stop multiple times to get his bearings and scrape the ice off the windshield. He was grateful his wife had convinced him to use the last of his severance to buy a car with four-wheel drive before they moved here.

Going over the events of his morning as he lay in bed shivering, Felix had to admit he should have just bought two bagels or two muffins at the bakery, anything to get a decent meal. But no, he had to go and get into an argument and then lose his shit at the gas station.

Elena had disturbed his sleep, and at this late hour, he found it impossible to stop his mind from tormenting him. Although he was beginning to feel pangs of regret for his rash behavior, Felix couldn't help but dwell on his miserable life. Unable to calm his restless mind, his thoughts turned toward his neighbor.

When he finally pulled into his driveway, exhausted but thankful he made it home in one piece, he habitually pressed the button on the garage door remote clipped to the visor. When he didn't hear the rumble of the motor, he remembered the garage door opener no longer worked. He couldn't afford to have it fixed.

Felix got out of his car, slamming the door behind him, and stomped over to the garage door. He bent down to grab the handle and noticed a fresh pile of turds in the driveway. He went ballistic.

Propelled by his rage, he slogged his way up his driveway and across the street through drifts of snow, fighting against the wind and snow that pelted his entire body.

He banged on his neighbor's door ready to punch him in the face.

"Open up, you bastard," he yelled.

Felix already resented his neighbor, who was too arrogant to bother saying good morning to him or his wife on his morning jogs. Once the dog began to use his property as a toilet, the neighbor became public enemy number one. Not to mention the little rat dog's constant yapping, which annoyed the shit out of Felix.

It didn't seem to matter how many times Felix complained, the neighbor didn't appear to care.

When the door remained closed before him, Felix shook his fist in the air and screamed, "If I see one more pile of shit on my property, I'm going to kill that fucking dog."

Woods galore around here for that mutt to fertilize, but no. He prefers to shit on my property.

On his way back down his driveway, Felix slipped and fell on his ass. Every time he tried to right himself, he skated for a few seconds and fell down again. Once he had finally slid his way back into the garage, he got back in his car and wept in frustration.

3
___

INSOMNIA

An hour later, Felix was still wide awake underneath the covers, mulling over his unhappy life. Although he finally felt warm enough to get some sleep, his mind was now filled with regrets—regret he'd moved to Pennsylvania after only eight months looking for work, regret he hadn't punched his former boss in the face for not warning him of what was coming before he was let go, regret he had married the wrong woman when he was young and full of lust and not much sense.

As he sank deeper into self-pity, his disappointment festered and grew, until he wanted to scream.

When it came right down to it, Felix had to admit Elena was right to be worried about him. These days he was always angry, drinking too much and yelling too much, his stomach always in knots. She had begged him to see a doctor about it, but he had refused. Perhaps he should consider her suggestion after all.

Thinking of his wife, dead to the world in the master bedroom, Felix knew she had been good to him, even though he hadn't always treated her well.

He'd married Elena for the sex. That's the truth of it. She

was beautiful, sexy, and game for anything during those crazy party days. Felix thought it would go on forever.

The thrill had worn off after the kids came, at which point Felix's wandering eye reactivated. He blamed his wife for not getting the weight off after the babies, for being perpetually tired, and as the years went by, he blamed her for aging. He could barely stand touching her, let alone having a conversation with her. He could hardly believe he was still married after all these years.

I'd go crazy if I didn't step out on her once in a while.

Meanwhile, he'd ignored the fact with each passing year, he'd also put on weight, his hair was thinning and graying, and the lines on his face deepening. It had never once occurred to him, perhaps his body no longer appealed to his wife either.

Elena looked past the physical and loved her husband just as much as she had during those crazy party days he longed for. Feeling responsible for taking him out of the city where he was happiest, she put up with his moods and did her best to make life bearable for him.

Still, any suggestion she made to get the love of her life out of his slump was met with a grunt. She was running out of ideas.

Felix, meanwhile, had become so wrapped up in his own misery, he failed to appreciate the one person who genuinely cared for him.

His depression had only grown when Elena persuaded him to move out of the city to a place where high-paying jobs were almost non-existent. She had painted a pretty picture of living among nature and starting a new life, but he suspected what she really wanted was to be closer to their son.

If ever he got a job in banking again, he'd be stuck with the kind of long commute everyone bitches about, all because he had given in to his wife in a moment of weakness.

A part of Felix was aware of his faults, and Elena had nothing to do with his discontent, but he was stubborn and resentful anyway. Feeling trapped, he couldn't help thinking it was too late to escape his wretched life.

He had been looking forward to going to the neighborhood bar that evening to persuade the owner to let him back in. He had a speech all prepared, but because of the blizzard, all he'd wanted to do was to get home intact. He would have to wait to plead his case.

Felix was as miserable as ever that night. Even worse, his wife had apparently decided the power outage would be the perfect opportunity for them to have a chat. As he listened to her relentless prattling, his annoyance only grew. He barely grunted in response.

"Felix, one of the customers at the salon mentioned she bought a 1920s ladies' dressing table at an antique shop in Stroudsburg. She said she loves shopping for antiques because she finds well-made items that have stood the test of time, as she put it," Elena smiled.

"Uh huh," replied Felix.

"She said there are antique shops all over the Poconos. She has a house full of vintage furniture and knickknacks she found in the area."

Felix took a sip of his beer, clearly not interested in Elena's customer and her love of antiques.

Elena waited a moment and said, "Maybe we can take a ride after the weather clears and spend an afternoon checking out the antique shops. Perhaps you'll find something you like."

Felix turned to her and said, "I doubt it."

"Well, you never know what you can find. I think it would be fun just to look, even if we don't buy anything."

Felix took another sip of his beer.

"We could stop for lunch somewhere—make it a day. It's been a long time since we've been out." She waited a moment, and said, "It would do us both good."

Felix offered a sarcastic, "Yeah," knowing antique shopping was never going to happen.

They passed an uncomfortable evening, Elena trying to engage him in conversation. She finally gave up and retired to their bedroom. Felix stayed downstairs brooding and hoisting beers until he felt sleepy enough to go to bed.

Although he didn't have to go to work the next morning, Felix wanted to get up early to shovel the driveway. He had been too exhausted to do it after his travesty of a day. Without some shuteye, he'd be dragging all day tomorrow.

Felix yawned noisily and sank deeper into the bed.

WHILE FELIX restlessly dozed on and off, someone headed toward his home intent on ending his troubles.

4

THE SLAUGHTER

He had barely fallen asleep again, when the sound of splintering glass abruptly pulled him back to consciousness. His eyes sprung open, heart racing. He strained to listen more attentively, wondering what could have woken him.

Did a tree branch break a window? Great! Something else to pay for.

Felix groaned as he sat up, drowsy from too little sleep. His bladder began to protest as soon as he swung his feet off the bed. Shoving his feet into his slippers, he trudged over to the guest bathroom and flipped the light switch, remembering belatedly, the power was out. Groping for the toilet in the dark, he relieved himself of the earlier beer binge.

Felix felt no urgency to confirm what he thought would be a costly repair job. Nevertheless, if there was a hole in the window, he knew he'd better cover it up before the storm brought in more cold air into his house.

Might as well see what the damages are. At this rate, I'm not gonna get much sleep tonight.

Carefully edging around the furniture, he felt for the flashlight on the nightstand, and again opened the storage bench to grab the last blanket. If the window were indeed broken, he would hang the blanket over the curtain rod to cover it, and hurry back to bed. He was too sleepy to look for cardboard and tape in the dark and cold basement. The blanket would have to do until morning.

Felix hurried down the stairs and across the small foyer, the blanket draped over one arm.

He stepped into the living room. Suddenly, everything went dark.

AWARENESS CREPT back to him slowly. He had no idea what had happened or how much time had passed. The throbbing in the back of his head overwhelmed his ability to think. Confused, he tried to remember how he had ended up on the floor.

Head throbbing, hands and legs bound, Felix began to thrash wildly as he tried to escape his shackles.

His restraints were as firm and impenetrable as ever when he stopped struggling a minute later, breathless from the effort. It was then he heard a menacing laugh.

The hairs on the back of his neck stood, as a shiver ran down his spine. He twisted his head in the direction of the sound, desperate to see through the darkness.

"Scream and I'll splatter your brains all over the walls. If you're thinking of calling for help, don't. I'll kill you quicker than you can get the words out, and then I'll kill your wife."

Oh no! Elena.

Felix would have wet himself then if he hadn't earlier emptied his bladder.

His captor fell quiet for a moment.

Felix's frantic mind worked at full throttle. In that brief pause, he tried to devise a plan to save himself and his wife. First, he needed to free himself. Then, he would charge the burglar as fast as he could, catching him off guard, and ramming him with his head. The burglar would lose his balance and fall backwards, giving Felix the opportunity to grab a fireplace tool and bash his head in.

Better yet, he would untie himself before the intruder noticed, and run as fast as he could to the bedroom. Locking the door, he would then call the police.

A moment later, reality sank in.

I'm tied up like a fucking calf. I can't run anywhere, and he'll kill me the moment I try.

"Pull yourself upright and lean against the wall," the intruder ordered.

Defeated, with great effort and a considerable amount of pain, Felix pulled himself into a sitting position. Panting, he leaned against the wall as best he could, heart beating a mile a minute, beads of sweat dripping from his forehead into his terrified eyes.

"I knew you could do it. Doesn't that feel better?"

Felix was in agony, the likes of which he had never felt before. His pounding head made him nauseous, and his inflexible body objected to even the slightest movement.

"In case you're wondering, this is not a burglary. I'm not here to steal any of your shitty possessions."

Is this a nightmare? wondered Felix.

His arms and legs tingled from the strain. Each time he tried to adjust his position to relieve the pressure, sharp bolts of pain shot all through his body.

"Do you like the color red?"

Red? Woozy with pain, he couldn't quite grasp the memories that flickered in the dark recesses of his mind.

Why is this happening to me? Oh God.

"Me? I love red, especially blood red."

Eyes wide in the darkness, Felix frantically tried to make out who had invaded his home. He *knew* that voice. If he could just think.

"Red, you idiot. That's a hint. Nothing? You stupid piece of shit. Perhaps I'll let you die without telling you why I killed you."

Felix tried to focus but couldn't break through the pain. His blood roared like a hurricane in his ears, his heart pounding and his breathing turning into ragged gasps.

He thought he heard angry whispers. Then, the distinctive sounds of a gun being loaded, sent fresh tremors throughout his entire body. Felix tensed and tightly closed his eyes.

Felix felt a searing pain as a surprising wetness gushed over his bicep. He swooned in agony, falling toward a dark abyss. Before the darkness could fully take him, however, Felix was jerked back to consciousness by the scent of ammonium carbonate rushing up his nostrils. He gasped and gulped in air, trembling, and deafened by the strangely magnified sounds of his every breath and heartbeat.

A phrase he once heard in a war movie floated through his mind with an odd clarity: *there are no atheists in a foxhole.*

For the first time since he was a kid, Felix prayed. *Oh God, I don't want to die. Please don't let me die.*

Despite his prayers, Felix found it hard to believe rescue was forthcoming from God or anyone else.

"Faint again and I'll shoot your other arm. I want your full attention."

"Finish it you creep," cried Felix in a hopeless attempt at bravado. "If you're here to kill me, just do it."

"You'd like this to end quickly, wouldn't you?" A rough fingertip traced down the length of his jaw. "*I'll* be the one to decide when it's time to end this."

Felix flinched, clenching his teeth, and stifling the scream that threatened to burst from his chest. "What do you want?" he forced himself to ask.

Silence.

Felix took a desperate chance.

"*Elena, help me!*" he croaked as loud as his parched throat would allow.

The backhand to his face snapped Felix's head sideways. "Fucking wise guy."

Felix felt the cold tip of a gun pressing against the side of his head. He shut his eyes and waited for the bullet.

A few endless seconds went by before Felix realized the gun was gone. He still could feel the phantom of its pressure against his skull.

He heard a rummaging sound from somewhere above him, followed by the unmistakable sound of tape being ripped from the roll. A dark figure bent over him close enough for him to feel a cool breath tickling his cheek. He squeezed his eyes tighter, terrified.

His eyes flew open again the moment the tape smacked down over his lips. He frantically jerked his head from side to side, roaring incoherently.

"Stay still and shut up you fucking piece of shit," growled his tormentor, backhanding him with enough force, he saw little light bursts in front of his eyes.

Felix had no more fight in him. He closed his eyes and helplessly endured the tape repeatedly applied to his face and around his head. He could barely breathe, hanging his head heavy with fear and exhaustion. He felt the slight air disturbance as his tormentor crossed in front of him. His eyes snapped open again at the sound of a heavy clang.

He began to thrash about in horror when he saw the poker raised high above him. He felt like he was watching a film in slow motion as the poker came whistling down in a sickening arc, landing squarely over his knees with a sharp crack.

The poker fell next to him on the carpet as he writhed and screamed in agony.

White, hot pain radiated from his knees throughout the rest of his body. His forehead erupted in a cold sweat, and his eyes leaked a steady stream of tears. If his mouth hadn't been covered, he would have awakened the entire neighborhood with his screams.

Upstairs, Elena's eyes fluttered halfway open at the sound of her husband's muffled screams. *Felix must be having a bad dream*, she thought, her mind still groggy with sleep. She turned over and fell asleep again.

In a state of shock, Felix slumped sideways until he dropped onto the floor on his injured arm. Lying there unable to move, he stared as the red blood saturated his wife's expensive white carpet. A strange calm overtook him.

White carpet was such a terrible idea. He began to laugh, guttural sounds like a wounded animal.

She fucked up.

"What's so funny?"

Felix gurgled.

"Ah. The carpet. Yes, I suppose the missus will be pissed when she sees it, but back to the business at hand. Do you know what a nasty excuse for a human being you are?" asked his captor, as though making small talk.

Felix was beyond listening. So great was his agony, words lost all meaning to him, and time ceased to exist.

"Hey you, pay attention."

Strong hands grabbed him by the shoulders and forced him back into a sitting position.

The fresh wave of pain brought Felix back to reality. *What have I done to deserve this?*

"I'm getting tired of this. Stop fucking around and listen to me. I have something to say to you."

Felix lifted his gaze just enough to peer into the darkness in the direction of the voice. He prayed the nightmare would be over soon.

"You destroyed a good thing with your foolish sense of morality. Was your betrayal worth it, you coward?"

The voice droned on, but Felix stopped listening. He thought of Elena asleep upstairs, and of his daughter and son. Sorrow and remorse overtook him.

His chin dropped to his chest. As he stared at the swollen

baseball-sized lumps where his kneecaps used to be, his last remnant of hope vanished. He was going to die tonight, that much was clear now. With his last bit of courage, he forced his attention back to the voice, hoping for a quick end to his suffering.

"...and that's why you're going to die."

Too dazed to understand, Felix could only stare, barely registering the clicking sound of a gun.

His soon-to-be killer approached, bending one knee, and placing the tip of a gun squarely on his chest. He peered through bleary eyes at the face before him, the specter's eyes boring into his own. Time skipped a beat as the executioner's face came into focus.

"Look hard, you bastard."

Felix's eyes widened in recognition. Flashes of memory flooded his mind. At last, he understood.

The killer smiled.

With a sense of relief, Felix Romero prepared himself to be liberated from the life he so scorned.

Duct tape was brutally ripped from Felix's face.

"Now's the time to beg for forgiveness. If you do, I'll let you live."

With his last ounce of strength, Felix looked directly into his killer's eyes. "Fuck you," he said right before his insides exploded.

Felix did not feel the furious assassin repeatedly spit his face, nor the angry kick to his mutilated body. He did not feel the soil flung to his face or realize a note had been left on his leg. The frigid air coming through the open door and shattered window did not bother him either. Felix was beyond suffering.

5

THE CALL

Sunday morning found many Pocono residents without power. The blizzard had raged all along the east coast, blanketing the area with twenty-three inches of heavy snow.

Residents who weren't lucky enough to have a generator or a fireplace, had wrapped themselves in winter coats and bedcovers, hoping their power companies would work quickly to get things up and running again. They made do with cold breakfasts, forgoing their usual cups of coffee or tea. Those who still had to work that day, shoveled their driveways and brushed snow from their cars, crossing their fingers the engines would turn over. The Pocono populace went about their day, oblivious to the horrific murder that had violated their quiet community while they slept.

One of their fellow Poconovians, as a popular local radio host called people living in the Poconos, lay dead on his living room floor.

A few miles away, I tossed and turned in my bed.

I watched solemnly as the medical examiner removed a tiny body from her mother's womb and placed it at a nearby table. The baby looked perfectly formed, like a doll.

The tiny corpse captivated me. I couldn't seem to look away to examine the mother's body more closely. Unable to focus, I stopped listening to the litany of observations the medical examiner recited. The only sound I heard, was the beating of my heart as it filled with a profound sense of melancholy I have never known before. The room slowly faded, all but for the beautiful infant robbed of life by her own father.

A strange paralysis seized my body as my soul filled with rage and sorrow. As I continued to stare, this perfectly formed creature, opened her eyes and looked directly into mine with a penetrating glare. In my mind, I heard a melodious infantile voice, ask, "Where am I? Where's my mommy?"

This was not the first time I'd heard her plaintive questions. I stood rooted to the spot, helpless, as I tried to find the right words. Just as I opened my mouth to speak, a loud and increasingly annoying noise distracted me.

My eyes sprang open, my heart thundering with a familiar grief. It took me a moment to realize it was the ringing telephone that had abruptly ripped me from my dream. Baby Matthews' questions would have to wait.

I stifled a yawn and reached for the phone. "Hello," I answered, my voice still groggy with sleep.

"Detective Pierce?"

"Yes."

"This is MCCC, Detective. There's been a homicide at 2223 Birdview Lane, off of Route 209 in East Stroudsburg. You're next on the list."

I wrote down the address on the pad I kept by the phone. "All right. I'll be right there. Thank you."

Louise gently grabbed my arm. "Is it a homicide?"

I turned toward her. "Fraid so."

"I'll keep dinner warm in case you don't make it back on time."

"Thanks, Sweetie. I was looking forward to having breakfast with you today."

"Me too," she murmured.

"I love you."

"Love you too," I said, and gently kissed her on the cheek.

She adjusted the covers and rolled over. I watched her for a minute, smiling when I heard her even breathing.

I had thought I would be sleeping in until 9:30 on this arctic morning. I'd left work early last evening because of the storm, holing up in my den and working on a cold case until well past midnight. I had been planning to enjoy a leisurely Sunday breakfast with my wife. All the same, it didn't surprise me when the ringing telephone roused me from a familiar dream. This happened more times than I can count.

I tore off the slip of paper and eased out of bed, padding down the hall to the den before dialing the district attorney. He promised to meet me at Birdview Lane as soon as possible. Stretching, I made my way to the bathroom.

Brushing my teeth, I found myself studying my weathered face. The deep lines etched around my mouth, forehead, and eyes, confirming my many years in law enforcement, witnessing the worst in humanity. I rubbed the stubble on my chin and cheeks. I needed a shave, but it would have to wait. I quickly splashed water on my face and ran a comb through my hair.

My eyes lit up with expectation as I prepared to go out into the storm, pulling on layer after layer of clothing. I was already looking forward to solving another homicide. You'd think after all these years, I'd be tired of it all, but I tell you, I love solving puzzles. That's what homicide investigations basically are. Puzzles of human pieces made up of ill-fitting edges.

I'm proud to be able to say, in my long career as an investigator, I have never failed to solve a case. I largely attribute my success rate to the meticulous work of my team. It also helps that most homicides are poorly planned, if planned at all. More often than not, the perpetrator will unintentionally leave something behind at the scene we can use to eventually connect the killer to the crime. Even microscopic particles from skin or clothing can often be identified and matched to an offender.

My mind drifted back to the Matthews' case. It never ceases to amaze me, we live in a world where a husband could viciously kill his pregnant wife without even considering the unborn child in her womb.

Child homicide investigations are the worst, as far as law enforcement officers are concerned. Every officer I've worked with has been filled with a similar sense of rage and determination to find those responsible when confronted with the grisly remains of a murdered child. It's not uncommon for child homicide cases to consume us with a depression that sometimes lasts well beyond the end of the investigation.

Out of all the gruesome child deaths I'd seen over the course of my career, it was baby Matthews who'd stayed with me ever since that vicious murder seven years ago.

The father, an insanely jealous and angry man, couldn't seem to make sense of the fact he'd stabbed and killed his wife. He had sworn up and down he loved her and would never hurt her, but the seventeen knife wounds on her body told a different story.

In his sworn statement, he admitted she had made him mad, and accused her of purposely trying to look sexy in her maternity clothes, to tempt other men. None of this surprised me—he seemed like the type. What astonished me was what he said next.

"I forgot my wife was carrying our child. I didn't mean to kill her."

Guess the creep forgot she was eight-months pregnant as he repeatedly stabbed her.

That case had been an easy one to solve. After unleashing his rage on his family, the sorry excuse of a man got drunk, cried for an hour, and then finally called 911. It's possible, had help arrived sooner, the baby, the mother, or both might have survived.

What has always stuck with me about that case is, even with all those random stab wounds, the fetus had not been harmed. He had punctured his wife's chest, arms, face, neck, and legs, but he'd stayed clear of her stomach. The prosecutor took full advantage of that fact and trashed the defense's insanity plea. Charged with a double homicide, he had no hope for parole, no matter how many times his lawyer appealed. As far as I was concerned, if there is one man who deserves the death penalty, it's Matthews.

I still wonder sometimes if his baby haunts him too.

I've never been able to offer baby Matthews a plausible explanation when she comes to me. How can I? The human race commits some of its cruelest atrocities when lost in the throes of emotion.

In any case, her spirit doesn't haunt my dreams so often these days. Sometimes months go by without a single visit. I think perhaps she's tired of my silence.

Soon, I was on my way to the investigation that almost ruined my perfect record.

6

THE KILLER

In a basement with windows heavily dressed in wartime black, sat Felix's executioner, ticking off a list of tasks completed, and tasks still undone. The light of a lone brass lamp, its incandescent bulb naked without a lampshade, illuminated the items spread across the table.

Shadows flickered on the basement's cold cement floor and cinder block walls, as a figure stooped over the heavily scratched antique table.

Long ago, she had spent hours familiarizing with shadows on the wall of a locked cellar, pretty much like this one. It was the only comfort she had as a child—that and holding tight to a tear-stained doll.

Felix's assassin quietly recited the completed tasks.

"Stain remover rubbed on coat, duct tape and latex gloves thrown in the fireplace, scoop washed, dried and back in the bag, smelling salts back in the first aid kit. What else? Oh yeah, hammer cleaned and put back in the toolbox. Clothes have been washed, dried, and hung neatly in the closet."

I'd almost forgotten to pick up the duct tape from the floor. Probably not important, but you can't be too careful.

These were the chores that had to get done as quickly as possible for obvious reasons.

Sleep was beckoning, yet adrenaline still coursed through her veins with thoughts of every delicious moment of the slaughter. Thinking perhaps fate had been at play, a smile appeared on her weary face, giving her a small shot of energy.

After all these years, we again cross paths.

A scowl replaced the smile almost as quickly as it appeared. He hadn't begged for forgiveness.

Son of a bitch!

Temporarily forgetting what remained to be done, she dragged the lamp closer. It was hard to concentrate when thoughts of the killing kept interfering. Despite the amount of pain she had put him through, the feeling he hadn't suffered enough to make up for his treachery kept slowing down the chores.

Felt good to spit and throw dirt on his stupid face. Sweet revenge.

Getting home hadn't been easy. The steep driveway had not been plowed or salted, making it difficult to climb. Being in shape had proven to be a plus.

Woulda been a sight if I'd fallen sprawled out and unconscious for the police to find. The assassin giggled at the thought.

Reaching for the coat and holding it under the light, she inspected every inch of the garment under a magnifying glass.

"Fuck." A rip showed under the glass.

Without another thought, she threw the coat on the floor on top of the wool hat, gloves, and boots. That pile would later be taken upstairs to be donated as soon as possible.

Now the best part—cleaning my treasure.

She picked up the weapon and began to quietly recite memorized instructions.

"Insert the magazine all the way. Twist the knurled knob at the breech a quarter turn to the left and pull back. Push the knob forward tipping a cartridge from the magazine into the chamber. When ready to fire, turn the knob one quarter to the right to cock the gun. Yes, practice is everything."

Shutting out the outside world while pushing down those persistent feelings of exhilaration, she disassembled the gun, placing every piece on the table with great care.

Disassembling and reassembling the weapon had become a favorite pastime over many years, ever since discovering it stashed in a trunk in the attic. A feeling of wonder had coursed through her entire body at the time of discovery.

As soon as I touched you, I knew you were meant for me.

One night, out of boredom and curiosity, she decided to explore the attic. She made sure her aunt was fast asleep, and quietly pulled down the chain to the folding stairs.

The attic was chilly, dusty, and smelled of old wood. She looked around, shivering, crossing her arms over her chest. She saw cardboard boxes of dishes wrapped in newspapers, some filled with novels she had no interest in reading. A couple of boxes of Christmas decorations that had never decorated the house in all the years she had been living there, were shoved into a corner. She went through everything, not finding anything interesting.

She inspected the matching set of luggage, still hoping to find something of value. Sitting on top of one of three suitcases, she opened the first one. It was filled with men's suits, ties, shirts, and two pairs of shoes. She closed that one, wondering whose clothes they were. She opened the one she had been sitting on, and saw it was filled with women's clothing, including two fancy evening dresses. *That old biddy had actually been young once. Hard to believe.*

In the pocket of an old sweater, she found some gaudy jewelry she kept, in case they were worth anything. In the last suitcase, she was delighted when she pulled out a long fur coat. When she tried it on, it was a bit loose, but kept her nice and warm.

Wrapped in the fur, she flipped the latches of a beat-up

steamer trunk. In it, she found a couple of old army uniforms and shoes, neatly placed on top of chenille bedspreads. She picked up the service cap and put it on her head, her imagination running wild.

Bundled in one of the bedcovers, she discovered the weapon, a manual describing the gun and all its parts, how to load it, and fire it. There was also a paper bag of bullets, and an envelope addressed to her aunt. She took out the letter from the envelope. It was from a buddy of her aunt's husband, written to her shortly after her husband was killed in the war. *She was married to a soldier?*

The buddy tracked her down and sent her the pistol her husband had carried with him in the war. His buddy offered to buy the weapon from her, thinking she must be hard up for money, and because he wanted it. Her aunt had apparently kept it because her husband wanted her to have it.

Thrilled with her find, she took out the remaining blankets to see what else was hidden within. At the bottom of the trunk, she found a pack of letters tied with string. At first, she thought they were love letters from the soldier to her aunt. Eager to read them, she undid the string and read the first letter. As she read, she grew angrier and angrier, When she had read all the letters, she tore them into little pieces, strewing them all over the attic floor like confetti.

That night, her already fragile psyche broke, and she began counting the days until her eighteenth birthday when she would be free.

The next night, and every night after that, she again climbed the stairs to the attic, put on the fur coat and army hat, and studied the notes for the gun. She could not smuggle the weapon out of the house to go practice at a firing range—she was only seventeen at the time and didn't know how to drive, and she couldn't very well shoot cans outside of her aunt's building. This was the city after all, not the country with a house and a backyard where you could shoot cans off a fence. It had taken her many months of practice to handle such a weapon without actually firing it, but the self-teaching had been worth the effort. A year later, having memorized every word of instruction, she took the manual, which was falling apart, and threw it in a street trash bin.

The lamp screeched against the table as the assassin dragged it closer to the disassembled parts. Picking up the barrel and reaching for the oil and cloth, she applied a thin, precise coat. She then lovingly inserted a cleaning brush and rotated it as if it were a living, breathing thing needing tender care, lest the bristles scratched too hard.

"Help!" interrupted a familiar voice.

The killer shrieked, dropping the brush and barrel.

Moaning, eyes shut tight, Felix's killer tried to close her mind to memories better left forgotten, but those haunting events of the past never asked permission to invade her troubled mind.

"She was a mean old bitch, just like your dried-up, miserable mother."

The killer began to sing Ozzie Osbourne's *No More Tears*, to quiet the voice in her head, and help shift her mind from those horrible years.

A tic developed at the corner of her left eye, but she kept singing.

By the time she finished her song, the memories had receded—the *voice* silenced. She went back to work, methodically cleaning and inspecting every inch of the firearm, fighting to keep the memories at bay.

A bead of sweat dripped down her neck as she confused the latest murder with memories of yesteryears.

"The look on his face when he knew me. I thought he was going to shit himself."

"You enjoyed that, didn't you?"

A two-way conversation with herself had commenced.

"I did, I did," the killer had to admit, fists banging the sides of her forehead.

"Your mother is dead, child."

"Please, be quiet," begged the tortured soul, though there was no one else in the room.

Once these two-way conversations arose, it was difficult for her to stop them.

"Come here, child. Take a handful of dirt and throw it into the grave. Go on now."

"No. I don't want to," the killer answered in a child's voice.

"It's your turn. Do what you're told," the *voice* commanded.

"She's going to beat me for throwing dirt on her," whispered the terrified child.

Her leg began to bounce under the table.

"They made me do it, Momma. Don't be mad."

"See? She didn't burst out of her casket. You're scared for nothing."

The killer pushed back the chair and jumped up, pacing back and forth across the room, trying to fight the memories.

"I'm going to cover her with a mountain of dirt," said the child's voice.

The past would not be stopped.

"What are you doing? Stupid child. You already threw dirt into the grave."

"Don't push me. I want to do it again."

The frantic killer stopped pacing and ran up the basement steps into the half bathroom off the kitchen. Sweaty and nervous hands yanked open the medicine cabinet and strained to twist off the cap on a bottle of aspirin. It popped open suddenly, spilling most of the contents into the sink. Hands still shaking, she rescued three tablets and swiftly swallowed them, with three Dixie cups full of water.

Standing at the basin for a few minutes with her eyes shut, she calmed down. The tired assassin stumbled back to the basement.

Her fingers moved swiftly for the next hour, but as exhaustion became too much to contend with, her eyelids flitted closed, her head slowly dropped to her chest and onto the table. Dreams instantaneously followed.

An old woman was speaking to her as a young child.

"Your mother died."

The smile on her face grows larger and larger until her face disappears, leaving only a stretched-out grin.

Scene change.

People shrouded in black, standing by a gravesite. The sky begins to fill with floating eyes. She can't help but stare at the many eyes in the sky as they blended into one giant eye, now focused on her.

She felt powerless to turn away. Then she heard the mourners.

"I think she killed herself—Mental illness. Shush."

She sees herself shoveling soil, packing the grave to overflowing.

Hushed whispers reaching her ears.

The killer moaned and twitched.

Scene change.

Two vague figures.

"I love you so much."

"Don't ever leave me."

A siren wails in the distance.

A door slams repeatedly.

A gun blast.

The killer's head snapped up off the table. Sweat poured down her anguished face—small pieces of metal gun parts stuck to her wet skin.

How long have I been asleep?

She plucked the pieces off her face and put all the parts into a box. Picking it up, Felix's assassin lumbered up the stairs and shut off the light, aching for sleep.

7

CRIME SCENE

I do my best to approach each homicide without assumptions, keeping myself open to all the possibilities regardless of what family, witnesses or friends might say about the deceased. Every investigator knows, if you put ten people in a room and create a crime in front of them, you'll often get different accounts of what actually occurred.

A scrupulous sleuth considers all the evidence from the scene of the crime, including statements from witnesses, neighbors, and interested parties. You never know where a crucial piece of information might come from. Sometimes, a seemingly innocuous remark, turns out to be the lead needed to clinch an arrest. Everything is important in a homicide investigation, and as detectives, we rely on facts, years of experience, and gut feelings. Trusting hunches, or hinkies, as we like to call them, have pointed many of us in the right direction.

I turned the corner onto Birdview Lane. The snow-laden pine trees lining the street looked as though they were bowing in reverence to the tragedy that had befallen their neighborhood. The beautiful houses, each dressed in white, made for a picture-perfect scene that felt at odds with the morning's events.

I parked my Subaru on the street behind a line of police cars and stepped out into snow, my eyes stinging as the frozen air blasted me in the face.

I could see a flurry of activity going on behind the police tape that surrounded the Romero residence. Static crackled through the air as the response team barked orders into their radios.

One of the officers slogged his way up the driveway toward me. It took me a moment to place him as Patrolman Alvin Cruz, beneath his many layers of heavy winter gear. Recently transferred from Miami, Cruz was clearly still acclimating to the brutal northeast winters.

Cruz greeted me with a smile. "Good morning, Detective."

"Morning, Officer."

"I brought you some coffee," he said, holding up the cup in his mittened hands to show me.

I reached for the cup, delighted but concerned.

"Hope you like it black."

"I do, but where did you get the coffee, Officer?"

"I... ah...I keep a thermos and a couple of disposable coffee cups in my car," he stammered, looking every bit as though I'd caught him with his hand in the cookie jar.

"You didn't give any coffee to the folks securing the scene, did you?"

"No, Sir. I know better than to contaminate a crime scene. I saw you arrive and hurried to get you a cup before you could get any closer to the property. It's brutal out here," he explained nervously.

"I appreciate that, but you know bringing coffee to a crime scene is against protocol."

Cruz lowered his head. "Yes, Sir. Won't happen again."

I felt a little sorry for the young police officer who, I was sure already realized he bent the rules.

I nodded my gratitude as I took a sip of the surprisingly strong, hot coffee.

"Let's talk inside my car," I said, getting in and turning the key in the ignition to get the heat flowing.

"So, what have you got for me?" I asked once we were settled.

Patrolman Cruz lowered his scarf and took off his mittens. He stowed them in a pocket before taking out his notepad and opening to the relevant page.

"The body of Felix Romero, a fifty-eight-year-old Hispanic male, was found tied up, tortured, and shot twice. The body was discovered by the victim's wife, Elena Romero, at or around eight ten this morning," he began his report. "She thought he was asleep in the guest bedroom. Apparently, he was snoring, so she threw him out of their bedroom between eleven and eleven thirty last night," he said, a slight smile appearing at the corner of his mouth. He suppressed it quickly and continued his report.

"Mr. Romero was employed as a delivery driver at Mariano's Pizzeria over on Courtland. Although he wasn't scheduled to work on Sundays, his alarm clock was set for eight AM, as he was planning to get up early to shovel the driveway. The Romeros did not own a snow blower," he explained.

I did my best to subdue my amused smile. It was clear Cruz takes his job seriously. He'd written down every bit of information exactly as told to him by Mrs. Romero.

Cruz again referred to his notes and read, "Mrs. Romero went to wake her husband when the alarm rang. As soon as she opened the bedroom door, the cold air shocked her. She headed straight to the guestroom to complain, thinking he had forgotten to keep the pellet stove going. When she didn't find him there, she immediately went downstairs. That's when she discovered his body."

He turned a page and continued. "She hesitated for a moment, and then hightailed it upstairs, where she locked herself in the bedroom and called 911. Dispatch clocked the call in at 8:14 AM. According to Mrs. Romero, she didn't go near her husband's body."

Cruz paused, looking up at me to see if I had any questions. I nodded for him to continue and took another sip of coffee, enjoying its comforting warmth.

"Based on what we've seen so far, we believe the perpetrator smashed in the dining room window, entered the premises, killed Mr. Romero, and left through the front door, leaving it wide open. Firearm has not been recovered. No perpetrator has been apprehended, and nothing of value seems to be missing. Mrs. Romero is too distraught right now to give us an inventory, but we're assuming, burglary was not the motive here."

He referred back to his notepad. "There are a couple of footprints still intact, leading from the broken window to the living room. They look like they were made with boots. Makes sense in this weather," he said, looking up from his notes and laughing.

"Got that right," I agreed.

"Lots of snow fell during the night. Any footprints left by the perp outside the home are now history."

I nodded.

Cruz cleared his throat and turned another page. "The police entered through the open front door when they arrived. They radioed dispatch once they got inside to let Mrs. Romero know police were here. She had refused to hang up until they arrived. After much coaxing, she unlocked her bedroom door to speak with us."

I gazed through the windshield at the house. The curtains were drawn on the lower level, as were the blinds on the second level. In the little while I had been there, I was already working the case.

"The forensic team is here and doing their preliminary assessment," Cruz said, closing his pad. We have officers questioning the neighbors as well."

"Anything else?"

"Mrs. Romero was processed for powder residue and bodily fluids. She claims she hasn't changed out of her pajamas and bathrobe since last night. She's clean."

"Where is Mrs. Romero now?"

"She's in the kitchen with Officer Durand. Safe zone has been set up from the back door of the house for investigators to walk through without disturbing the scene."

"All right, Al. Thanks."

"Yes, Sir," he nodded, stashing away his notepad, and pulling his mittens from his pocket.

"Oh, Al, before you go, would you do me a favor?"

"Anything, Sir."

"Wait here a moment."

I swallowed the last of my coffee and put my cup in the holder before getting out of my car. Opening the trunk, I rummaged through my toolbox and pulled out my twenty-five foot builder's tape measure. Gesturing for Cruz to come join me, I walked over to the top of the driveway.

"Stand right here and hold this for me while I walk down to the garage, please. I want to see how long the driveway is," I said, handing the tape measure to Cruz and taking hold of the tape end.

The driveway was steep and icy beneath the snow cover. Determined not to humiliate myself in front of the young cop, I took my time going down, following the deep footprints that had been left by the police before me. I almost slipped a couple of times, but thankfully recovered.

I was almost at the bottom when the tape ran out. I estimated the driveway to be about twenty-eight feet, more or less, a long way to see through a frosted window during a blizzard. Anyone watching from that distance or further, would not have been able to see clearly. Perhaps with binoculars or a telescope they would have been able to see movement inside, assuming the lights were on, but that still wouldn't have helped much.

I jotted down the measurement in my notebook. Since I was near the garage, I rubbed the frost from the window and took a peek inside. I could just make out a dark colored SUV. I wrote the information in my pad and began the trek back up. I was maybe halfway up when I slipped on an icy patch, my feet flying out from under me. I barely managed to hold onto my pen and pad, as I landed on all fours. It took me a couple of tries to make it to the top, red faced, wheezing, and sweating from the exertion.

To his credit, Patrolman Cruz displayed no amusement on his face when I reached him, leaving me a shred of dignity at least.

I hurriedly thanked him for his help as he handed me the tape measure.

"If there's anything else I can do for you, Detective, please let me know."

"Will do. Thanks again."

I unfurled my scarf as soon as Cruz turned to leave, letting it hang around my neck, and undoing the top button of my coat, I was tempted to take my hat off too, until I remembered my wife's dire warning that exposing a warm head to cold temperatures, was the perfect recipe to catch a deadly flu.

I watched, envious, as the young officer deftly made his way down the driveway like a sure-footed mountain goat. At his age, I too would have thought nothing of the possibility of breaking my bones hurrying down a steep, icy, driveway.

Popping the trunk once again, I put the tape measure into the toolbox and took out my prized digital Nikon from its protective case.

It's the forensic photographer's job to document the site and surrounding area of a crime scene for evidence before anyone has a chance to disturb it. As thorough as they are, I like to take my own pictures as well. It gives me a more personal sense of the scene and everything and everyone around it. Later, I'll incorporate my own pictures with what the forensic photographer shot, for a more detailed study. Judging by the activity going on at the house, the photographer had already finished.

I slammed the trunk shut, deep in thought, as I hung the camera around my neck and turned toward the house. If the intruder had been surveying the area, perhaps someone would have noticed a car idling nearby.

I began snapping pictures of the crowd of onlookers across the street, standing on the frozen sidewalks in their pajamas and overcoats, shivering but too curious to go back inside. These photographs might prove useful if we later connected a suspect to one of the bystanders casually speaking to police.

I crossed the street, scouring the road for any tire tracks or rubbish that might have suggested a stakeout from a parked car. Nothing. The cars along the street were buried in enough snow to make it obvious they hadn't been moved since the storm began.

I overheard the neighbors' whispered comments as I walked by, methodically snapping pictures of the residences on either side of the victim's home and the ones on my side of the street.

"What happened?"

"I think someone got killed."

"Didn't really know them, but I heard she's nice."

"Maybe she killed *him*."

"Were they robbed? They won't tell us anything."

Two police officers moved through the crowd, taking statements, and jotting notes in their pads. I nodded greetings as I passed up and down the block, all the while keeping the Romero house in sight.

When I was satisfied I'd covered every aspect of the immediate vicinity, I returned to the Romero property and carefully navigated the driveway. Almost fell again, but thankfully, I made it down intact.

The porch lamps were turned off and no automatic light

activated as I shoe-skied my way toward the garage. The killer had been fortunate. Not only had they chosen a moonless night with heavy snow, but the lack of illumination from the porch and the driveway, would render the trespasser virtually invisible.

I circled around to the side of the house and stood in front of the breached window, imagining the break-in. The first thing I noticed were the overgrown bushes in front of the window. They created a convenient hiding spot.

Studying the point of entry, I took a few photographs from different angles and examined the jagged edges of the window for any signs of blood or fibers from a torn piece of clothing.

I crouched down, carefully combing the ground to see if anything had been buried by the snow during the night—a cigarette butt, piece of gum, anything that could be used to match DNA. Still, I found nothing.

I continued to click the Nikon as I slowly moved toward the rear of the house, turning my head in every direction as I looked for clues.

When I reached the back door, I inspected the locks for any signs of tampering. There were two locks. The first was a typical low-quality builder's lock, and the second one wasn't much better. The intruder had chosen to enter the house through the side window despite the rear door offering better concealment and a quieter entry. Perhaps the killer didn't know how to pick a lock, I speculated. In any case, the stormy night would have been thunderous enough to chance breaking the window.

Looking out over the back yard, I saw no roads or paths that led to the back of the house, just woods covered with undisturbed snow as far as I could see. I made a mental note to check a topography map of the area when I got to the precinct.

I now had the lay of the land and enough photographs of the exterior to study. With that, I entered the Romero household.

8

INITIAL THOUGHTS

The temperature inside felt only a few degrees warmer than outside, not that it made a difference with the wind freely circulating through the shattered window and open door. Another round of photographs from the entryway and I was ready to study the scene.

Patrolman Peter Durand stepped through the back door and joined me. "Good morning, Detective."

"Morning, Pete. I understand no one other than Mrs. Romero was in or around the premises when the police arrived this morning."

"That's right, Sir."

"I noticed the looky-loos have been kept at a distance."

He smiled. "Yes, Sir."

"I didn't see any press."

"No, but the paper might send someone over later."

"See they're kept back, please."

"Yes, Sir"

"Thanks, Pete."

I walked over to the living room entrance. Lying on the ground a few feet apart were a heavy blanket and a flashlight that was still on. CSIs had already placed markers by the items.

Flashlight makes sense, but why the blanket? For warmth?

I stepped inside the room, scrutinized the area to get a feel for what might have happened. There were lots of family pictures on the walls. I paused to study what looked like an aged wedding portrait of a young, good-looking couple, presumably the victim and his wife. Beside it hung a smaller, more recent-looking photo of another young couple. The bride in the second photo bore a strong resemblance to the woman in the first.

Luxurious white carpet and expensive-looking brown leather furniture filled the spacious living room. Neatly stacked women's magazines on the coffee table next to a few burnt-out tea candles in a dish. Opposite the sofa, stereo equipment and a flat screen hung over a wooden credenza where a few more family pictures were displayed.

The surface of the credenza was covered in ring stains and scratches that marred the otherwise beautiful wood.

On the far corner of the table top, set apart from the picture frames, was one bottle each of vodka, rum, and tequila, each of them almost empty. A few glasses were haphazardly arranged nearby.

Next to the sofa was a large, comfortable-looking recliner. There were three empty Yuengling beer bottles on the floor beside it.

I noticed a pellet stove by the wall near the entrance to the dining room. At the moment, the stove was not emitting any heat. A fireplace tool set rested beside it with one piece missing. A foot away and to the side of the stove, someone had positioned a dining chair.

I stood behind the chair and directly in my line of vision was the victim. As I took in the scene, I spotted the missing poker lying beside the deceased.

Careful to stick to the path marked for the walk through, I

approached the crime scene investigators who were busy processing the incident. Mr. Romero's body would not be moved until they finish, and the coroner officially declares the victim deceased.

"Hi fellas."

CSI Seager squatted on the floor closely examining the body. She straightened up at the sound of my voice. "Hey, Howard."

"Hi, Kate. What have you got so far?"

"Victim was taken down with a blow to the back of the head where there is extensive bruising, then trussed up like a turkey while unconscious. His hands and ankles were bound with twenty-four and thirty-six-inch zip ties."

She bent down and moved the body forward a little to show me his hands. "As you can see, the ties are tight enough to have cut into his skin."

"I see. This is no ordinary break in, is it?"

"Seems not," Kate answered, standing again. "We're hoping once the ties are removed, we'll be able to determine if any usable prints were left behind. We've processed the poker near the corpse, most likely used to crack his knees. The only prints we found on the chair belong to the Romeros. Matter of fact, we haven't been able to find any prints other than the Romeros. The assailant most likely wore gloves."

"Yeah," I agreed.

"Two shell casings have been recovered consistent with the two GSWs on the victim, as well as the nine-millimeter bullets."

"That marker over there," she said, turning and pointing, "indicates a bullet was fired from approximately the same distance away from the corpse as the dining-room chair."

She turned back to face the body. "As you can see, there are no powder burns on the victim's arm," she said, pointing to one of the gunshot wounds. "That shot went clean through."

"And the second?"

"That's the kill shot, delivered directly to the chest. There are burns on the garment and what's left of his torso. The bullet most likely ricocheted off the spinal column and exited on the upper left side of his back, taking out the shoulder. As you can see, there is significant tissue loss at the wound's site."

"What can you tell me about the dirt on his face?"

"Eyes open, indicating the dirt was flung on his face after death. We've taken a sample for testing, but it looks like ordinary potting soil to me."

I snapped a closeup of Mr. Romero's face before scanning the rest of the body.

"What's that paper on his leg?" I asked with interest.

"Note left by the killer, we assume. The paper is clean, indicating it was placed there after the slaughter."

I snapped a full-body picture before bending to get a closer look at the note. "Have you ever seen anything like this?" I asked as I snapped a close-up.

Seager shrugged. "Looks like doodles to me."

"Me too, but it definitely means something to the killer." I stared at the strange scrawl a moment longer. "Any defensive wounds?"

"None that I can see. We've bagged his hands in case any traces of his assailant are on them or underneath his fingernails. I didn't find any fresh scratches or other signs of a struggle, but perhaps the medical examiner will find something after washing the body."

"Perhaps. Anything else?"

"We photographed a couple of footprints right inside the window that were still somewhat distinguishable. They measure somewhere close to a size eleven-wide boot. Lucky for us, the prints had probably iced up by the freezing wind coming in through the broken window and open door."

"We also found a fiber on a shard of window glass. Could be from an overcoat, hat, or scarf." A mischievous grin spread across her face. "It's pretty raw out there to be out killing people in your birthday suit."

"That it is, Kate. That it is," I laughed.

"We'll know more after the postmortem and lab results."

"Any blood on, or around the shattered window?"

"No, but if the killer cut himself and touched the victim perhaps he left us a present."

"We should be so lucky," I said, smiling.

"Coroner should be here soon. We'll let you know when we're finished."

"Thanks."

I snapped a few more pictures of the area around Mr. Romero's body before making my way to the stairs leading up to the second floor.

Assuming the killer broke in to murder only Mr. Romero, it was feasible he would have looked for him and either tortured and killed him in the guestroom or killed both Mr. and Mrs. Romero in their bed. Since the torture of Mr. Romero appears to have been important, the missus would likely have been killed immediately had they been in the same bed.

The element of surprise as well as the raucous storm would have been in the killer's favor. Then again...

Maybe Mr. Romero had already been awake when the window was smashed in.

Was the blanket meant to cover the window?

Mr. Romero may have gone downstairs to investigate after he heard the glass shatter, which would have delivered him right into the assassin's hands. Mrs. Romero didn't know how lucky she was, that she had thrown her husband out of their bedroom when she did.

Climbing the carpeted stairs, I counted twelve steps from the bottom to top. The killer would've had to hear Mr. Romero coming, and think fast in order to lie in wait. Maybe Mr. Romero had coughed or cleared his throat on his way down. Or perhaps the perpetrator was already heading upstairs when he heard the victim, or saw the beam from the flashlight, and rushed downstairs to hide.

The laminated floor between the bedrooms, creaked beneath my feet.

I made a left and felt a comforting warmth wash over me when I entered the master bedroom. The small fireplace provided the only warmth in the house. I was tempted to go stand in front of it, though the fire had burned down to embers. I glanced around the room and reluctantly walked out.

Heading in the opposite direction down the hall, I reached for the door to the guestroom. I pulled it open and closed, open and closed, listening as it creaked on its hinges.

9
___

ELENA

I headed back downstairs and made my way to the
kitchen. Before approaching the widow, I stood in the
entryway and studied her. She was sitting at the kitchen
table in her winter coat, a scarf wrapped around her head and
neck, and an afghan covering her lap, as she spoke with
Officer Cruz. Listening to her voice, I picked up an undertone
of panic and noticed a slight trembling in her gloved hands.

*Either that woman is on the verge of collapse, or she's an exception-
ally good actress.*

Cruz noticed me in the doorway and waved me in. "Mrs.
Romero, this is Detective Pierce. He's in charge of the investigation. I'm going to step outside and let the two of you talk. I'll
be back to check on you later."

"Thank you," she said, her voice hoarse.

"Hello, Mrs. Romero. Thank you for taking the time to
speak with me," I said, as I sat down across from her. She
nodded in response, her eyes downcast. "I know you've been
through a terrible ordeal, and have already told the police…"

"Oh my God. I can't believe Felix is dead," she interrupted,
sobbing.

I offered her a tissue from the box on the kitchen table.

"It's a terrible thing, Mrs. Romero, but we'll do everything in our power to apprehend whoever did this."

I waited for her to dry her eyes before continuing. "I hope you don't mind a few more questions."

She tucked a strand of hair under her scarf and took a shaky breath. "I just want this day to end," she said, her voice trembling.

"I understand. I'm deeply sorry for your loss."

To put her at ease, I began the questioning with a compliment. "You have a lovely home. How long have you lived here?"

Her face imperceptibly brightened. "Almost two years."

Mrs. Romero wadded the tissue in her hand and shoved it into the paper bag next to her.

"A lovely home in a very nice area. Are you friendly with your neighbors?"

"I say hi to them sometimes, but that's all. Felix doesn't interact with them very much."

"No? Why's that?"

"I mean, the man across the street made him mad because his dog sometimes does his business on our property, and when Felix complained, he didn't believe him."

"Any problems with anyone else?"

"Not really. Most of our neighbors have jobs. No one really has the time to get to know each other. You know how it is."

"Yes, I do. It's sometimes difficult to make friends. Outside of the neighborhood, did your husband have any friends he saw on a regular basis?"

She shook her head. "Oh, no. Felix isn't very friendly. Not since we moved here, anyway. When we lived in New York he went out with his coworkers sometimes."

"Oh yeah? Where to?"

"Where? Oh, maybe to a ballgame, or a bar. Every once in a while he'd take me along to see a movie with his colleagues and their wives, or to a work event, and sometimes to a nice restaurant," she said, blinking away the tears that threatened to escape her eyes. "He was happier back then. I think losing his job turned him into a different person."

"How so?"

"Well, he complained about everything once we moved here. The lack of good jobs in this area, the neighbors, the cold, the high electric bills, even our house. He said it creaked a lot. You name it," she shrugged. "Poor Felix. I tried to convince him to get involved in some community activities, but he was never interested. He's always been a bit of a loner, to be honest."

"I see. Is there anything you can remember about last night you haven't told the police? Anything at all that might help us in our investigation?"

"There's nothing more to tell. When my alarm went off this morning, I tried the bedside lamp to see if the electricity had come back. It hadn't yet, so I grabbed the flashlight and went to wake Felix. When I opened my bedroom door, I was shocked it was so cold in the house. When I didn't find Felix in the guestroom, I figured he was downstairs already checking the stove. Oh God."

Mrs. Romero began wringing her hands, her tears spilling over and making tracks down her cheeks. She covered her eyes and curled into herself, rocking back and forth in her chair.

I gazed at Mrs. Romero as I waited for her to calm down. She had a melancholy aura about her I suspected had been there long before her husband was murdered. The creases around her swollen eyes did nothing to detract from their beautiful shade of brown. She had the longest eyelashes I had ever seen, though they were currently clumped together with tears. Despite her red and puffy face, swollen from so much crying, and her uncombed, graying hair, it was easy to see she had once been a beautiful woman.

When she cried herself out, she dried her eyes, blew her nose, and adjusted the scarf around her head.

"Take your time, Mrs. Romero. I know this is difficult." She gave me a watery smile.

"I was certain Felix would've filled the stove before he went to bed. He complains constantly about the drafts in this house, so he always makes..." She gulped. "He *made* sure," she corrected herself. Her eyes took on a faraway look.

"Such a strange feeling in the pit of my stomach," she said, her voice so low I had to lean forward to hear her. I've never felt that kind of cold before. It scared me for some reason. I tried to convince myself Felix had to be downstairs checking the stove."

"Has the stove ever run out of pellets before, on a particularly cold night?" I gently coaxed.

"What?" She blinked and gave her head a small shake, as though waking herself from a trance.

"Oh, no. It doesn't make any sense. The stove should have been working. Felix keeps it filled. He's adamant about saving electricity. We depend on that pellet stove to keep most of the house warm."

"I noticed you have a wood-burning fireplace in the master bedroom." She nodded.

"The pellet stove isn't strong enough to warm the bedrooms upstairs. We're lucky the people before us had that fireplace built. Electricity is expensive in the Poconos." She paused, perhaps realizing she had echoed her husband's number one complaint.

"Good thing there's so many trees on our property, that we never have to buy wood. Otherwise, I'm sure he would have had us sleeping downstairs, she said, smiling wistfully. Of course, we do have to buy bags of pellets, but Felix figured it's cheaper than paying a huge electric bill."

"I guess the pellets burned faster because of the wind

coming in through the broken window and open door," she mused, her brow furrowed.

"That makes sense. Did you notice anything unusual before you found your husband?"

"Yes, the front door was wide open. I was halfway down the stairs when I saw it. I panicked and started to run, calling for Felix. I almost tripped over the flashlight when I got to the entrance of the living room. I looked to see what I had kicked and saw the flashlight and the bedspread."

She took a deep breath before continuing. "I couldn't understand what they were doing there, or what Felix must've been doing. The more I tried to make sense of things, the more frightened I got. I kept calling out for Felix, but of course, he wasn't answering," she said, lowering her head.

"Then, I went into the living room and, I...found him," she said, her voice cracking.

"What did you do next, Mrs. Romero?" I prompted, after a long, silent moment.

She began to twist the tissues in her hand.

"At first I wasn't sure what I was seeing. I pointed the flashlight on him but had to look away. I couldn't believe it was Felix." She closed her eyes and shook her head.

"He looked like a filthy...wounded...animal, and he was dead. I knew that, but part of me wouldn't let me trust what I was seeing," she said, her voice choking off as she gulped back a sob.

"I'll never be able to get that picture out of my mind." She looked at me with haunted eyes.

"What did you do after that?"

She took a deep breath before answering. "I couldn't move, but then it suddenly hit me. The killer might still be in the house. I ran upstairs as quickly as I could and locked myself in my bedroom."

"You were right to protect yourself. Did you call the police right away after that?"

"Yes. I picked up the phone on Felix's nightstand and called 911. I wouldn't hang up until they arrived."

"You did the right thing, Mrs. Romero," I said, giving her an encouraging smile. "Now, I want you to think back. Did anything disturb you during the night at all? Did you hear anything unusual, for instance?"

"Nothing I can remember, except..." She suddenly looked horrified. "Sometime during the night, I thought I heard Felix scream."

I perked up. "You heard your husband scream?"

"I think so. Sometimes Felix has vivid dreams as if he were fighting with someone. He gets quite loud. I thought he was having another nightmare, so I went back to sleep." Her eyes widened as she realized what she had just said.

"Oh my God. I should have checked on him when I heard him scream," she moaned, dropping the tissues, and covering her face with her hands.

She abruptly pushed back her chair and stood, ignoring the afghan that slipped off her lap, and walking over to the windows. Deep, mournful sobs shook her entire body.

I got out of my chair and helplessly stood by, giving her time for that much needed release.

When she was done, she turned her wet and tormented face toward me. "I'm sorry. I didn't mean to do that."

"Please don't apologize, and don't blame yourself. You had no way of knowing your husband wasn't having another nightmare."

Just then, Patrolman Durand stuck his head in the door. "The coroner's here and so's the D.A.," he announced.

"Thank you, Officer."

I picked up the blanket. "Mrs. Romero, please sit."

She reached for the afghan and sat. When she had gotten herself settled again, I offered her the box of tissues.

She wiped her eyes and blew her nose, taking a deep,

shaky breath, before turning her attention back to me. I nodded encouragingly before asking my next question.

"Mrs. Romero. I want you to try and remember. Did you happen to notice the time when you heard your husband's scream?"

She shook her head, "No. Like I said, Felix often talks in his sleep. I'm used to the nightmares, but I can't help thinking maybe I could have saved him."

"If you had gone to check on him, you probably would have been killed too. It's fortunate you were used to your husband's bad dreams."

With a pained look, she blinked away fresh tears. "I know, but I wish I would have checked on him. Maybe I would have heard something and called the police. Maybe he'd still be alive..." she trailed off, her eyes taking on a distant look.

"It does no good to dwell on what you did or didn't do. You are not to blame for what happened to your husband. The person who broke into your house is the only one responsible."

Mrs. Romero silently blinked away her tears of guilt.

"It's all right, Mrs. Romero. I understand how you feel. The best thing you can do for your husband now is to try and remember anything about last night that could help me catch the person responsible for your husband's death."

She nodded, and sat up, ready to cooperate once again.

I gave her a sympathetic smile.

"Anything unusual happen last evening before you went to bed?"

"Unusual? Not really, except for the power going out while we were watching the news."

"And around what time was that?"

"Oh, somewhere around nine fifteen, nine thirty. The local news was still on when we lost power."

"Did you and your husband go right to bed at that point?"

"Not at first, no. The lights had been blinking on and off for most of the evening, so we'd been expecting the power to go out sooner or later. Felix had gotten a couple of flashlights from the kitchen and put them on the coffee table, and I got out the tea lights. I thought the power outage might be a good opportunity for us to chat, but he didn't feel like talking. After a while, I gave up and left him alone. I was already in bed by the time he came upstairs."

"And you remained in your bedroom all night?"

"I did, yes, but like I told you, Felix was snoring, and I asked him to sleep in the guestroom."

"And that was sometime after eleven last night?"

"I think so."

"All right. As far as you're aware, was there anyone who might have had a reason to harm your husband?"

"Felix? No, no one. He has a temper and yells at people sometimes, but I don't think anyone would kill him over that, do you?"

"That's what we're going to find out."

"Are there any places Mr. Romero frequented? Social clubs, bars, a billiard hall maybe, any place where he would go to unwind after a hard day's work?"

"He sometimes went to BB's Tavern for a beer, but I don't know if he had any friends there." I nodded, jotting down the name of the bar.

"I also have to ask, and you'll pardon me for the question, but do you know if your husband was having an affair?" Her jaw tightened as she looked away.

I held my breath.

Avoiding my eyes she struggled to answer. "No... no...I mean, when we lived in the city, I suspected he was fooling around sometimes. I never confronted him though, so I can't say for sure," she said, her voice dropping down to almost a whisper. "He would have denied it anyway and he probably would have turned it around on me," she said, her eyes downcast.

"How so?" I urged.

She lifted her chin and looked straight at me. "Felix always said I was jealous. Called me all kinds of nasty names. That's what he did whenever I challenged him on anything. He's never been good at taking criticism."

Suddenly she looked stricken. "Oh, I shouldn't be talking badly about my husband. I'm sorry."

"No need to apologize. I know you want to catch your husband's killer as much as I do. Please, go on."

She hesitated.

"It's all right, Mrs. Romero."

"I don't think Felix was fooling around," she blurted.

"What makes you say that?"

"He didn't have the money to take a woman out. And anyway, I would have known. A woman always knows."

I decided to see if I could push her just a little further.

"Has anyone ever contacted you with allegations your husband is, or was romantically involved with someone else?"

She looked surprised by the question, like I had discovered a secret.

"No," she said a bit too forcefully.

My gut told me there was more to this, but I could tell by her stiff spine and crossed arms, I wasn't going to get anything more from her about it.

"Just a few more questions. You wouldn't happen to remember if the porch or driveway lights were turned on last night before you lost power?"

"No, neither. Felix turns them off when he gets home. We don't even have a nightlight if you can believe that. Like I said, he was adamant about not wasting electricity."

"Are there any firearms in the house?"

"Firearms?" She looked surprised.

"Yes, any guns in the house?"

"Oh no, we don't own any guns. We've never even talked about guns."

"All right. Last question. "Why is there a fireplace tool set by the pellet stove?"

"That's a housewarming gift from a friend. We already have a set for the fireplace in our bedroom, so we didn't need another one. My friend doesn't know the difference between a fireplace and a pellet stove," she said with a smile. "She's lived in New York all her life and doesn't know how a pellet stove works. Felix has been using the brush and shovel from my friend's gift to clean the stove, so it worked out."

Her eyes were beginning to glaze over, she was running out of steam.

"Thank you for speaking with me, Mrs. Romero. Do you have anyone you can call to come and stay with you?"

"Yes, the young officer already called my children. My son lives in Allentown. He should be here soon. My daughter is flying in from California today or tomorrow."

"All right. In the meantime, I'll ask Patrolman Cruz to stay with you until your son arrives."

"Thank you again for speaking with me. You've been very helpful. If you remember anything else, no matter how trivial, please tell Officer Cruz, or ask for me."

I picked up my camera and walked out. Catching Cruz's attention, I waved him over, and sent him back into the kitchen to watch over the grieving widow.

10

EXPERTS

The district attorney, pale and wide-eyed, held a handkerchief over his mouth, watching the coroner examine the body.

"Hello, Stan," I said, as I walked over.

"Oh hey, Howard," he said through the hankie, tearing his eyes away and looking grateful for the distraction.

"You okay?"

He lowered his hand from his mouth and let out a tremulous breath. "I'll be fine once I get out of here. Seen enough gore for one day."

"Yeah. This one's bad."

"I'll say. Keep me up to date on your investigation. Whoever did this, is a maniac and deserves to be locked up."

"Will do."

He stowed the handkerchief in his pocket and turned up the collar of his coat.

"Bye all," he called, hurrying out without waiting for a response.

Can't say I blamed him.

I wanted to get the coroner's thoughts. "Another nasty one, Bob. What do you think?"

The coroner twisted his neck and looked up.

"Oh, hello Howard. Give me a sec," he said, making another note before he rose.

"This is an obvious one, Detective. The perpetrator took down the deceased with a blow to the back of the head, shot him through the right arm, and smashed his kneecaps. They finished him off with a bullet to the chest. A cold-blooded execution, but not before the killer took some time to torment his victim. Not too much time though. He hadn't completely bled out before the fatal shot."

"Time of death?" I asked.

"Core body temperature indicates his body heat dropped rapidly after death, which makes sense given the frigid atmosphere of the house. The reddish-blue discoloration of the skin suggests livor mortis developed at least one and a half to two hours ago. Hard to tell when rigor began, if at all. It's minus twenty Celsius in here. Rigor mortis most likely would have been developed much quicker than the twelve hours it would normally have taken at room temperature. Do you have some sort of timeline?"

"Wife says she last saw her husband alive between eleven and eleven thirty last night."

"What time were police called?"

"The call came in at eight fourteen AM."

"Okay. Judging from the damage this man suffered, window for time of death would have been between midnight last night and eight this morning. The ME will get you a closer TOD after the post-mortem. I'll pronounce him deceased at…" he glanced at his watch. "Time of death, nine fifty-two AM."

"You guys can move the body whenever you're ready. I'm done," the coroner called to the techs.

He peeled off his latex gloves, stowed them in a pocket and rubbed his hands together. "I'd shake your hand, Howard, but mine are ice cold." He smiled. "I'll call the morgue. See you next time."

"Thanks, Bob. Keep warm."

"You too, Howard."

He tugged on his Russian-style hat and put on his gloves.

"You guys almost done?" I asked the techs.

"Just about," answered Seager.

"All right. I'll meet you outside after the body is moved to the ambulance."

I went back into the kitchen. Mrs. Romero was once again standing by the window, hugging herself and slowly swaying. Cruz stood nearby, ready to spring into action should Mrs. Romero faint.

"Mrs. Romero," I called out. "We're ready to take your husband to the Lehigh Valley morgue."

She gave no indication she'd heard me.

"Mrs. Romero?"

Just then Fernando Romero dashed into the room.

"*Mami!*" he called, making a beeline toward his mother, and scooping her into a hug. Mrs. Romero threw her arms around her son's neck, burying her face in his chest and bursting into tears again.

"*Nando, mataron a tu padre,*" she said, her voice muffled.

"I know. I'm here now. I'll take care of everything," he said. He looked up and nodded in my direction, gently extricating himself from his mother.

"Sit, *Mami,*" he said, walking her back to her chair and tucking the blanket around her legs. "It's really cold in here. Can I get you a cup of tea?"

"No, Nando. I don't think we're allowed to touch anything."

"Oh. I'll make you a cup as soon as everyone leaves," he said, rubbing her back and moving the tissue box closer to her.

"All right." She sniffled and reached for another tissue.

"I'll be right back. I want to speak with the detective."

"*Si, Hijo.*"

Fernando gently kissed his mother on the cheek and turned to me.

"Are you the one in charge?"

"Yes. I'm Detective Howard Pierce."

"Can we step outside, please?"

"Sure."

"Goodbye Mrs. Romero," I called out. "I'll be in touch."

Fernando waited until we were out of earshot of his mother before asking, "Have you any idea what happened to my father?"

I briefly filled him in, leaving out the more gruesome details.

Fernando's face grew pale, shaking his head in disbelief.

"I'd like to ask you a couple of questions before I leave, Mr. Romero."

"Sure. Anything."

"Where were you last night between the hours of midnight and eight AM?"

"I was at an anniversary dinner that turned into a party. Didn't get out of there 'til two this morning."

"Go alone?"

The corners of his mouth twitched upwards. "No, not alone. I brought a date. Lucky for me she got stuck in my apartment when this awful storm hit."

With his deep voice and tall and trim body, not to mention his full head of hair, it was easy to imagine him dating a lot.

"Can anyone corroborate that?"

"Yes, of course. I can give you a list of the people who attended, as well as the name and address of the young lady I'm seeing."

"Where was the dinner?"

"In my apartment building in Allentown. Any farther, and I wouldn't have been able to make it there in this blizzard," he joked, an easy smile on his face.

I nodded.

"Girlfriend live in Allentown too?"

"Yes." He reached into his pocket and pulled out his wallet. "Here's her business card with her information. She's a professional photographer; works out of her apartment."

I took the card and glanced at it briefly before tucking it into my wallet and pulling out one of my own. "Here's my information. Please call me with that list."

"Absolutely."

Behind him, I saw the body bag being lifted onto a gurney. It was time for me to get going.

I was about to shake his hand and make my excuses when Fernando spoke again.

"I'll be staying here tonight, of course, and probably for the rest of the week. I don't want to leave Mom alone until we figure out what to do next." He ran his fingers through his hair and blew out a breath.

"As much as I want to take my mother out of here, until I can get the house back to order, I doubt I'll be able to drive her to a hotel in this weather."

"All right then. I'll know where to contact you."

"Where are you taking my father's body?"

"The coroner has ordered an autopsy hoping to recover potential evidence. I'll be escorting him to the morgue in Lehigh Valley."

He blinked away sudden tears and said, "I better go move my car so you guys can get out. There was no place to park, so I left it in the middle of the street. Don't want you guys giving me a ticket," he added with that same incongruous grin.

His smile faded as he took in my stony expression. "Please keep me informed," he said, turning up his collar and holding out a hand.

"I will," I promised, as we shook.

I let him get a little way up the driveway before following, hoping to avoid another embarrassing performance. I was grateful to make it to the top without falling this time.

I quickly brushed the snow off my car, cursing myself for not warming it up before the ambulance was ready. I had just gotten in, when the ambulance took off, forcing me to follow in my unheated car.

HOMICIDE VICTIMS TAKE priority at the morgue. The medical examiner was waiting for us when we arrived. Owing to the vicious manner in which Mr. Romero was murdered, the post-mortem took a little longer than usual.

Once the exam was finished, I had just one more stop to make before heading to the precinct.

11

BRIEFING

I stepped into the supercenter and smacked the snow off my coat, pulling my gloves off and shoving them into my pocket. Enjoying the warmth, I tugged my scarf loose and looked around. The place was a ghost town — no more than a few brave souls walking the empty aisles. No doubt, they were regretting not having prepared for the storm. I turned my head toward the couple of unhappy cashiers and smiled. They barely acknowledged me.

Ok then. I made my way to the back where a friendly face greeted me.

"Hey, Detective Pierce."

"Hi Charlie. I was hoping you'd be here."

"Oh yeah. No reason for me to miss work. I live on Orchard Street, close enough to walk."

"You're a brave man, Charlie. It's freezing out there."

"Nah, it's invigorating," he said. "Plus it's good for my weight," he added with a laugh, patting his ample stomach.

"So, what can I do for you?"

"Can you get these developed right away?" I asked, taking out the rolls of film from my pocket and placing them on the counter.

"As you can see, I'm not busy at the moment," he laughed, gesturing to the nearly-empty store. "So yeah, I think I can develop those films for you."

"Guess I came at the right time. Thanks pal."

"I should be thanking you, Detective. You broke my boredom."

"Glad I could help."

"Regular three by fives?"

"Yes, please. Oh, and Charlie," I said as he picked up the rolls of film and started to move away from the counter. He paused and looked back at me.

"There's a picture of a note in there. I'd like five copies of that one, please."

"You got it."

"Just a heads up, some of the pictures are pretty gruesome."

"How long have you been coming to me for this kind of thing, Detective? I'm used to it by now. Don't you worry about it."

"These are particularly shocking."

"I appreciate the warning, but like I said, no worries."

He went directly to the back to do his work, and I wandered into the electronics department next to the photo center to pass the time. I heard the whir of the photo machine a moment later. Before I knew it, Charlie was calling me back over.

"Done so soon?" I asked.

"Told you. Not busy," he smiled.

He handed me two envelopes. I peeked inside the first one, swiftly checking all the ghastly photographs in living color, before setting it on the counter. Reaching inside the other envelope, I pulled out one of the copies of the note. Happy with the clarity of the image, I shoved it back into the envelope and set it on top of the other one.

"As usual, these look great. Thank you," I said, handing him my credit card.

"Any time," he replied, his expression troubled.

"I'm sorry you had to see those, Charlie."

"It's okay. I just never seen anything like that. Looks like the poor guy was butchered by a crazy person."

"Yeah. Don't you worry though, we'll get him."

"I know you will, Detective." He slid over my card and receipt.

"Thanks. See you soon."

"Good luck with your case."

"Thanks again."

I hoped he wouldn't have nightmares after this. *Perhaps I should learn how to develop my own films.*

———

"GATHER AROUND GUYS," I called as I entered the squad room.

Once everyone had left their desks and was grouped around in front of me, I began the briefing.

"A fifty-eight-year-old Hispanic male is tortured and gunned down in the middle of the night in his home with a nine millimeter, probably with a suppressor, since neither his wife, nor the neighbors heard the gunshots." I paused, to make sure I had their full attention. Satisfied, I continued.

"The bullets and shells recovered at the scene were consistent with the two gunshot wounds suffered by the victim." I sneezed.

"Bless you," yelled the crowd.

"Excuse me. I think I'm catching a cold."

"Here, Sarge." Detective Hanley, the youngest member of the team, offered me a packet of tissues. He had been a medic during the Desert Storm War and was used to caring for people. He had a drawer full of remedies for whatever ailed you, even a fever thermometer. At first, Hanley got ribbed for keeping a portable pharmacy in his desk drawer, but there wasn't a member of the team who at one time or another hadn't gone to Detective Hanley for a cough drop, band aid, aspirin, or temperature check.

"Thank you, Kyle." I took a moment and blew my nose.

"Now, where was I? Oh, yes. Leaving shells behind probably means the firearm had been wiped of all identifiable markings, or he thinks we won't be able to trace it back to him. With that in mind, I think it's safe to assume this was not a professional hit. According to the ME, the victim was knocked unconscious by a blow to the back of the head, most likely with the butt of a handgun or a tool of some kind. His hands were bound behind him with zip ties. Ankles were also bound."

The room was filled with the scratching of pens on pads as everyone jotted down notes.

"We believe the fireplace poker found near the body is the weapon used to shatter Mr. Romero's knees. The only fingerprints found were from the Romeros. There were traces of an adhesive around the victim's mouth, face and even in his hair, presumably from duct tape or similar. The tape itself was not recovered. There was also a pool of saliva between the victim's chin and neck. We think the killer might have spat on the victim. If that's the case, the sample should be able to tell us more about the killer."

"Let me get this straight," interrupted Ignacio Ramirez, my second in command.

"The killer left no fingerprints and made sure to take the duct tape, but he didn't care about leaving brass behind?"

"Can't think of everything, Iggy. You know how it is," quipped O'Malley, always quick with the sarcasm. "Too many things to think about when you're trying to outsmart law enforcement."

"If I may continue, gentlemen," I interrupted before the conversation could get derailed any further. "The victim was shot through his right arm, but he didn't completely bleed out at that point. The killer seems to have tortured him for a brief period of time before taking the final shot."

"The perp entered the home through a dining room window and left through the front door. Crime scene investigators found a fiber on a window shard. They also took a picture of a footprint that approximates a man's size eleven wide. A search of the premises revealed no valuables or souvenirs were taken. It seems the killer's sole intent was to torture and kill Mr. Romero."

"Corporal, would you pass these around?" I asked, handing Ramirez the stack of photos of the victim's mutilated body.

My team was made up of seasoned detectives, most of whom have seen many gory homicides in their careers, but that didn't mean they were immune to the shock of a gory crime scene. Detective Byrne let out a low whistle as she flipped through the pictures.

"The assailant left some kind of message on the victim's shin," I continued when the photos had made the rounds. I motioned for Ramirez to give out copies of the note, which proved to be a welcome distraction from the gruesome pictures the group had just seen. As expected, the team had plenty to say about it.

"Looks like my three-year old drew that," said O'Malley, our class clown.

"Nah, I think you did, O'Malley," said Hanley. "Not bad for a forty-year-old."

"Hardy, har-har. You wish you were that talented," O'Malley responded.

"Looks like some sort of shorthand," observed Ramirez.

"What makes you think so?" I asked. All eyes were now on Detective Ramirez.

"My aunt was some kind of secretary in the sixties. She's always writing herself messages in shorthand. This looks a lot like those scribbles."

"Does she live nearby?"

"Tobyhanna."

"With the condition of the roads, best you scan the note and email it to her. She does have email, right?"

"Oh yes, Sir. She may be old, but she's not intimidated by technology."

Everyone laughed.

"Good. If it really is some kind of shorthand, perhaps she can help us decipher it."

"I'll get on it soon as we're done here."

"Thank you. In the meantime, please check PaCIC and NCIC databases in case a similar note turns up."

"Yeah, yeah," they mumbled. I smiled at their annoyance. There was really no need to remind this bunch to check the databases.

By this time, I had a slight headache. I pinched my nose to alleviate the pressure in my sinuses and stifled another sneeze before I resumed.

"Another interesting detail for you. We found soil on the victim's face, thrown there after death. Could be some kind of ritual. Any ideas?"

They had ideas!

"Maybe it's the killer's way of saying Mr. Romero would soon be in the dirt," said Celia.

Laughter filled the room.

"What? I'm *serious*," she insisted.

"Or maybe the killer's calling him a dirt bag," added Leung.

Ramirez chimed in. "Maybe it's a civic-minded killer. He wanted to contribute soil for the burial."

His suggestion brought on another bout of laughter.

"All right, all right," I said, reeling them back.

"Could be a way for the killer to say goodbye," said O'Malley, once they had settled down again.

"What do you mean, Sean?" I asked with interest.

"You ever seen a funeral where the mourners each throw a handful of soil in the grave?"

"Sure."

"You don't see that too often anymore, but it used to be quite common. Nowadays, the gravediggers usually don't lower the casket until everyone has left—too many fainting relatives."

"Is this an Irish ritual, Sean Brody O'Malley?" asked Detective Byrne in her best Irish brogue, and a wide grin splashed across her face.

O'Malley was unfazed. "Not necessarily, the custom actually originated in Israel. I've seen it at Irish Catholic funerals too, and a friend of mine who is Lutheran, also observed this practice, so I don't think it's only indigenous to Jewish people."

"Ooh, indigenous," exclaimed Detective Hanley. "Been playing Scrabble with your kid again, Sean?"

"You're just envious, cause your sad, illiterate ass can't put two words together without a dictionary," O'Malley retorted.

The room exploded with laughter once again.

"All right, all right, let's reel it in team," I said. "O'Malley, it's a plausible theory, but we'll have to learn more about the killer before we can be sure."

O'Malley nodded in agreement.

"The autopsy confirmed Mr. Romero expired from a direct gunshot to the heart. No defensive wounds and no traces of the perpetrator left on the body. Let's hope the lab results will give us something useful."

Everyone diligently wrote down the pertinent information.

"There's probably plenty of gun owners in the area who own nine millimeters. Let's check PICS and see if that leads anywhere. We'll start there and expand the search if need be. The ballistics report will tell us more. The size of a footprint right inside the breached window, tells us we're probably looking for a male suspect about five ten."

"Or a tall female with big feet," suggested Byrne.

"Yes, Ceci, or a tall female with big feet," I added, smiling, and shaking my head.

Preliminary briefing over, I blew my nose and moved on to assigning tasks.

"Ramirez, please interview the owner of Mariano's Pizzeria where the deceased was employed. Byrne, you dig into the Romeros' financial records. According to Mrs. Romero, our victim liked to unwind at BB's Tavern."

"I'll drop by the bar to see what I can dig up on Romero," I said, already anticipating a smart-alecky remark.

Hanley took the bait.

"And for a beer, Sarge?"

"Very funny," I answered, straight-faced. "I want to talk to the owner, get a feel for what kind of person our victim was."

I paused for a moment. "*Then* I'll have a beer."

"Better make it a hot toddy, Sarge," he recommended. "You don't look so good."

"Good idea."

"The rest of you, work on putting together a picture of the kind of person Felix Romero was. I'll interview the neighbor Mr. Romero threatened about his dog. We'll discuss our findings tomorrow morning and see where we stand. Let's dive into Felix Romero's life and let him lead us to his murderer. You know our motto…"

"*To solve the mystery, start with the victim!*" they chorused.

"All right, guys, pack it in for today. This storm does not seem to be dying down anytime soon. Drive safely. I'll see you all tomorrow."

"Go home and take care of that cold," yelled Hanley, waving goodbye.

I headed outside and cleared the snow from my car, cranking up the heat to full blast as soon as I got inside. Head pounding from the pressure in my sinuses, I couldn't stop coughing the entire way home.

12

THE SIBLINGS

I went straight home, where Louise pampered me with medicine, hot tea, and soup. She set up a steam inhaler near me and forbade me from getting out from underneath the covers.

I was still under the weather the next morning, despite having slept through most of the night without coughing. Louise brewed me a cup of strong tea with lemon and honey for breakfast, insisting I eat some toast as well, despite my lack of appetite. While I ate, she filled me in on the goings-on at the senior apartments where she volunteers.

When I was ready to go, Louise would not let me out of the house until she had taken my temperature and fed me a spoonful of cough medicine.

Although I was maybe a little annoyed at all the fuss over me, I'm grateful for the love and attention I receive from my wife. Watching Louise pamper me, I marveled that after thirty-two years of marriage, she still pulled at my heartstrings.

THE ATMOSPHERE on Birdview Lane felt eerily quiet compared to the hustle and bustle of the previous day. I glanced over at the Romero residence and saw the porch lights were lit, as well as every room on the lower level of the house. Evidently, power had been restored to this neighborhood.

A white van with the lettering, GREEN CLEANING & JANITORIAL SERVICES on the side was parked in front of the garage. Naturally, the family had hired a cleaning service after the crime scene was released. They would, of course, want to get rid of the bloody evidence congealing on their living room floor, a grim reminder of the terrible way their loved one was tortured and murdered.

Fernando Romero's Lexus with the vanity plate FROMERO, was parked next to it, and behind the Lexus was another vehicle I assumed to be the daughter's rental.

I rang Mr. Adler's doorbell twice. No answer. I'd wanted to interview him about the quarrel he and Mr. Romero had concerning the dog.

Not wanting to waste the trip, I decided to drive across the street to see if either of the Romero children could shed some light on their father's habits. I was pleasantly surprised to find the driveway had been plowed and salted. I pulled in and parked behind the van.

A pretty young woman with red rimmed, and suspicious hazel eyes answered the door when I rang the bell. I recognized her from the wedding portrait hanging in her parent's living room.

"Yes?"

"I'm Detective Howard Pierce," I said, flashing my identification. "I spoke with Mrs. Romero yesterday. I have a few more questions if I may."

"Ah yes, of course. I'm Margarita Diaz, her daughter. Please come in, Detective."

"Thank you," I said, stepping inside.

"I am very sorry for your loss, Mrs. Diaz."

"Thank you."

"How is your mother doing?"

"Not great. Won't come downstairs until the living room has been cleaned. It's been quite traumatic for her as you can imagine. She had nightmares last night, and now she's afraid to go to sleep."

"I'm sorry to hear that."

"Thanks."

"Did you just get in this morning?"

She nodded. "I just got here maybe an hour ago. I flew in on a red-eye from California."

"That's a rough trip."

"It is, but I'm glad I didn't get here until after they got started on the cleaning. My brother wasn't able to get anyone to come out yesterday because of the storm. Thankfully, he was able to get someone to come out this morning."

"Yes. I saw their truck parked outside."

"My brother's in the kitchen. I'll let him know you're here. Perhaps we can answer some of your questions."

"That would be helpful, thank you."

"You can hang your coat there," she said, pointing to a coat tree to my left. "The dining room's straight ahead, please, make yourself comfortable while I go get my brother."

She had excellent posture, I noticed as she walked away, with her head held high and her shoulders back. Perhaps she was a dancer or an athlete?

As I walked past the living room where Mr. Romero was slain, I paused for a moment to watch the cleaners at work. There were two men on the job, one of who was patching the wall where Mr. Romero's body had leaned. The other was busy running the shampoo machine back and forth over the white carpet. The blood residue could never be fully erased, I knew, although it could be cleaned well enough to be invisible to the naked eye.

The damaged window in the dining room had been boarded up, the floor cleared of broken glass. Someone had filled the pellet stove. It really did warm up the house quite comfortably.

Fernando emerged from the kitchen. "Ah, Detective. We meet again," he said, raising his voice over the noise of the cleaning equipment. We shook hands.

"Excuse me a moment, would you please?"

He strode into the living room with a self-assured air of authority, waving over the worker who was scrubbing the carpet, and speaking to him quietly. The man nodded, shut off the machine, and motioned for his partner, the two of them disappearing into the kitchen.

"That's better," said Fernando as he came back to the dining room. "My sister tells me you have more questions?"

"I do. I'm trying to put together a picture of your father's normal activities," I explained.

"Please sit, Detective." He pointed to the chair across from him. "Margarita is bringing us some *café con leche* and cake."

"Please, don't trouble yourselves," I said, pulling the chair out and sitting.

"It's no trouble at all," he said. "The coffee's already made, and Mom had some cake in the kitchen from some bakery she's always raving about. I was just about to cut myself a piece when Margarita told me you were here."

"I'll have some coffee then. Thanks."

"By the way, I wrote down the names and addresses of the people at that anniversary bash I was at on Saturday."

He pulled out a folded piece of paper from his shirt pocket and passed it to me.

"Per your request."

"Thank you." I unfolded the paper, taking a cursory glance at the names before setting it aside. I'd look more carefully later.

"Ah, here she comes," exclaimed Fernando as Margarita appeared in the doorway with a tray.

"Coffee, Detective?" she asked, setting the tray on the table.

"Thank you." I nodded as she passed me a cup.

"Cake?"

"No, thank you. I don't think my stomach can handle cake at the moment. I'm just getting over a cold."

"Would you prefer a cup of tea, Detective?" she asked.

"Oh no, that's okay. Coffee is fine."

"Are you sure? It would only take a few minutes."

"That's kind of you, but really, coffee is fine."

"Do you take cream and sugar?"

"I take it black, thank you."

Margarita was smiling politely, yet I couldn't help but notice she was a little shaky when she poured my coffee. She served a cup for her brother and sliced a piece of cake for him.

"Come sit, Margarita" said Fernando, patting the chair next to him. "Let's see if we can help the detective."

Margarita perched herself awkwardly on the edge of her seat, her back stiff and straight, and her hands twisting nervously in her lap. Fernando, on the other hand, leaned back comfortably in his chair and took a leisurely sip of coffee, as though he didn't have a care in the world. "How can we help you?" he asked me.

I glanced at Mrs. Diaz and saw more than sadness in her expression. She seemed distinctly uncomfortable.

"Did your father have any bad habits?" I began, getting right into it. "Gambling, drugs, booze, anything where he might have been involved with people who might try to hurt him?"

I could tell my first question had affected Mrs. Diaz, by the way she averted her eyes. I was disappointed when her brother was the one to answer. I would have liked to know what she was thinking.

"No, no," said Fernando, shaking his head. "No gambling, no drugs. My mother did complain about his drinking though.

She claimed he drank when he was unhappy, and lately, he was always unhappy."

"Why do you think so?" I asked.

"He'd been depressed ever since he lost his job at the bank, but it got a lot worse when they moved out here. Mom said he hadn't been sleeping very well, and apparently got into the habit of drinking himself to sleep. She tried to warn him about alcoholism, but of course, he didn't listen."

I wondered if perhaps he had been on his way downstairs for a drink on the night of his murder.

"Do you know if he had any friends or coworkers he used to drink with?"

"That I don't know, but I suspect he did most of his drinking alone. He wasn't very sociable," he said, with a wry smile.

"I see. Do you know if your father owned a firearm?" I asked.

"No. I was trying to convince him to learn how to shoot. I even offered to buy him a gun and pay for shooting lessons so he and mom would know how to protect themselves if someone broke in, but he wouldn't listen." He shook his head. "I wish I'd been able to convince him. Perhaps he'd still be alive."

"You can't blame yourself. Owning a gun doesn't necessarily protect you. In some cases, a firearm in the home can actually be used against you."

"Perhaps, but at least it gives you a fighting chance."

"I take it you're a gun owner?"

"Yes. I own a Glock Seventeen."

"Do you have a permit?"

"Yes, Sir. In my wallet."

"What about the gun? Have it on you now?"

"Always."

"Mind if I take a look at your firearm and permit?"

"Why do you need to see his gun, Detective?" Margarita blurted, before he could answer. "Are you insinuating my brother killed our father?" She glared at me, arms crossed tight over her chest.

"I'm sure Detective Pierce is only doing his job," Fernando quickly said, hoping to soothe her.

"Really? Because from where I'm sitting, he seems to be making unfounded accusations," she retorted, without taking her eyes off of me.

"Margarita, *por favor*," he pleaded.

"I'm not here to offend anyone," I said, meeting her gaze, "but I do have a job to do, and I will conduct my investigation as I see fit, Mrs. Diaz. Now, let me ask you this, assuming your brother did not assassinate your father, wouldn't my inspecting his gun disqualify him from my list of suspects?"

Mollified, she took a deep breath and sighed. "I apologize, Detective. I just can't believe..." she trailed off, pressing her trembling lips together as her eyes teared up and spilled over.

"It's all right. I understand," I reassured her, before turning back to Fernando, who was looking sadly at his sister.

"Now, if you don't mind, may I please inspect your weapon and permit?"

Fernando bent down, drawing the Glock from underneath his pants leg. He proudly held it out to me.

This guy probably fancies himself some kind of cop. Perhaps he thinks it's cool to holster his weapon at his ankle, cutting reaction time if he needs to retrieve it in a hurry. Bet he thinks he impresses the ladies when he shows off the holster.

Fernando walked over to the closet and came back with his wallet, pulling his permit out and setting it on the table next to the gun.

I took my time examining the weapon, glancing at Romero every once and again to see if he showed any sign of nervousness. He appeared cool as a cucumber, completely unbothered, taking a huge bite of cake, and gulping it down with the last of his coffee. Only Margarita seemed apprehensive.

"Wow, this is really good cake," said Fernando. "Sure you won't have a piece, Detective?"

"No. Thank you."

He finished his slice in two more bites.

I took out my pad and scribbled a few notes, before handing the Glock back to him. I wrote down the info from his permit and handed that back as well.

"Thank you, Mr. Romero."

"No problem." He bent down for a moment and reholstered the gun.

"What line of work are you in?"

"I'm a technical consultant."

"What exactly does that entail?"

"I have a degree in Information Technology and Computer Science" he said, pouring himself another cup of coffee. "I help businesses develop IT systems so they can grow efficiently and profitably," he proudly said.

"As long as I keep up with the latest computer and networking trends, I can walk into any company, do an analysis of their computer system, and advise the owners of any changes that would be beneficial to their business. Most of the time it means enhancing their networks in one way or another."

"Who is your present employer and where is the company based?"

"I'm an independent contractor. Companies hire me as an outside consultant."

"Do you do much traveling?"

"Yes. I travel all around the northeast. Some companies run their businesses out of their factories in remote sections of town. Hence the gun."

"How long does a typical contract last?"

"That depends. Some companies have antiquated systems that require a complete overhaul. Those contracts can last anywhere from a couple of months to half a year or so. Others just need upgrading, which I can sometimes do in as little as a week."

"Sounds interesting," I commented, looking up from my notes.

"It can be," he said, reaching for more coffee.

"Are you on a contract currently?"

"I'm actually between assignments, but I'll be working in Philly next month for a company called Then To Now Innovators."

I jotted down the information before turning toward his sister, whose impatience was etched all over her face.

"What about you, Mrs. Diaz? What do you do for a living?"

She took a breath, exhaling slowly. Was she just trying to control her emotions, or was she really that frustrated by my questions?

"Why does that matter, Detective? How is knowing my profession going to help you catch my father's killer?"

Is she going to object to all my questions?

"Until this crime is solved, everyone is a suspect. Please answer the question."

"Now hold on a minute. You can't seriously believe my sister had anything to do with our father's murder," objected Fernando, clearly annoyed.

"You never know when a simple question will lead to a breakthrough in a homicide investigation," I answered, without taking my eyes off of Mrs. Diaz.

"I work at the middle school in San Dimas," she answered, exasperated.

"What do you teach?"

"I teach modern dance."

"Yes, I suspected from your posture you might be an athlete or a dancer," I said, nodding thoughtfully. Her face flushed.

I picked up my coffee and took a slow sip to buy myself a

moment to think. Why was Mrs. Diaz giving me such a hard time? I wanted to get to the bottom of her resentment.

"What does your husband do for work?"

"He's also a dance teacher, an exceptionally good one," she answered."

"Really? What's his name?" I asked, amused.

"He's not famous yet, but one day the dance world will know his name, Joseph Diaz," she said, her head held high and proud.

I wrote the name in my pad, indifferent to her prediction of her husband's fame.

"Now, I have to warn you, my next question might be upsetting to you both. Are either of you aware of, or have ever suspected, your father of infidelity?"

Mrs. Diaz' left eye twitched ever so slightly in response. She brought her hand up to touch the area.

Now we're getting somewhere.

"I really don't know the answer to that, Detective. That kind of thing is between my parents," Fernando answered, smirking.

"What about you, Mrs. Diaz? Do you know if your father ever had an affair?"

Looking at her lap, she shrugged.

Margarita looked as though she was barely restraining herself from arguing with me again. Her expression became more and more resentful with every question I asked. Where was the animosity coming from? I decided to dig deeper.

"Tell me about your relationship with your father, Mrs. Diaz. Were you close?"

"What? How do you mean?" she asked.

"Did you love him?"

"What kind of question is that?" interrupted Fernando.

I ignored him and pressed on.

"I can see you're upset, Mrs. Diaz, but please answer the question."

"I'm upset, Sir, because my father was horribly murdered, and here you are trying to dig up dirt about our family."

"I'm looking for leads, not dirt," I stressed.

She rolled her eyes and looked away.

"Believe me, I want to catch your father's killer as much as you do. I apologize if my questions upset you, but it's a necessary part of the job. All I'm asking for is a little cooperation, please."

"I apologize, Detective," she said, abashed." I just don't want you to get the wrong impression about my dad," her eyes watery with tears.

"I understand. Now please, tell me about him."

"My father was no different than any other father. He worked long hours, and he wasn't always around, but he spent time with us whenever he could. And yes, I loved him very much."

"When did you move to California, and what made you decide to move?"

"I got married before mom and dad moved to Pennsylvania, almost three years ago. My husband grew up in California and always intended to go back after college. Before we got married, we visited San Dimas and I fell in love with it."

"How often have you visited since then?" I was surprised to see she looked stricken by the question.

In a shaky voice, she answered, "This is the first time I've come back." A tear escaped her eye and trickled down her cheek. She wiped it away with trembling fingers.

"Three years is quite a long time," I commented. "What kept you from visiting?"

"My husband and I have remarkably busy lives," she said, almost pleading. "We work all week at the school, and we give private lessons on weekends. The last time we took a vacation was our honeymoon."

"Really?" Fernando mocked. "What about that trip to the Grand Canyon?"

Margarita looked like she wanted to strangle him.

"Well, we've taken a couple of short trips, but never a real vacation is what I meant," she explained, her face turning a vivid shade of red.

"I see."

"One last question," I said, addressing Fernando this time. "I understand your father spent some time at BB's Tavern. Would you happen to know if he frequented any other bars or establishments in the area?"

Fernando shook his head. "Nah. Only place he went to drink was BB's, according to Mom, and that was only once or twice a week."

I nodded to myself, satisfied for the time being.

"All right, that's all for now. Thank you both for your time," I said, standing up and shaking hands with each of them.

I turned to Margarita.

"I'm sorry if I upset you, Mrs. Diaz, but like I said, the more I know about your father, the better I can build a case."

Fernando interceded before she could respond.

"Thank you, Detective. I'll see you out," he said, bustling me over to the front door and hurriedly putting on his coat. He ushered me out the moment I'd gotten my coat buttoned, closing the front door behind him.

"My apologies, Detective. I didn't want to bring this up in front of my sister. She adored our father. Of course she did, she was his princess, but the truth is dear old dad wasn't kind to our mother. Don't get me wrong, he didn't hit her or anything. Not as far as I know, at least, but he was mean to her. I don't know how she put up with it."

"I see. Is there anything else I should know?"

"My mother called Margarita once, after Margarita had already moved to California," he explained. "She told her she hadn't been happy in a long time, and she didn't know how to help Dad. Can you believe it? She was so unhappy, but all she wanted to do was help my father. My sister called and told me everything. She made me promise to check in on them every once in a while."

"And did you?"

"To be honest, I stayed away as much as I could. My father never really had much to say to me, and I couldn't stand watching my mother try to bridge the gap between us."

"Any reason for his indifference toward you?"

"Guess he didn't like me interfering when he snapped at Mom. Or maybe he just didn't like me," he mused. For a brief moment, I thought I saw sadness in his eyes.

"I did make a point of calling my mother every week for a while, but I've been calling less and less in the last few months. She complains about the same things every time, and, well, I guess I just got tired of hearing it. She only talked about Dad's temper and how guilty she felt for suggesting they move to Pennsylvania. I almost yelled at her last time I called. I wanted to tell her to just leave him, but I held my tongue. What was she supposed to do? She was totally dependent on him. She probably has no idea what to do now that he's gone," he said, his voice bitter. He paused for a moment to gather his thoughts.

"As for cheating," he went on. "There's not a doubt in my mind my father messed around. He was quite the asshole. You'll see after you speak with his neighbors," he finished, smiling ironically.

"I take it your father and you didn't have much of a relationship."

"No. It was like my sister said. He wasn't home very much while we were growing up, and when he *was* home, he only had eyes for her. I learned to take care of myself. Ever since I moved out, my father treated me like a guest of my mother's every time I came to visit. No, Detective, we did not have much of a relationship."

"Why didn't you tell me all of this inside?"

"You saw how she reacted when you asked about infidelity. It would only have upset her more to hear all this." I nodded.

"There's something I don't understand, Mr. Romero. If your sister loved your father as much as you say, why did she really stay away?"

Fernando sighed. "Margarita couldn't stand the tension between our parents, and it hurt her to see Dad's drunkenness. She kept in touch by telephone after she moved, but as time passed, she called less and less. Similar to what I did, I guess. I think for her it's a way of holding on to her childhood image of our father. She adored him."

"Is there anything else you want me to know?" I asked him.

Fernando was quiet for a moment, his gaze distant. He shook his head suddenly, like he was coming out of a trance.

"No, I just wanted to give you a full picture of who he was."

"I appreciate that," I said as we shook hands again.

Interesting interview, I thought to myself as I watched him stroll back inside.

————

A PAIR of narrowed eyes watched from behind the blinds, a finger holding down a single slat. Detective Pierce parked in front of Mr. Adler's home.

What's he want with that jerk?

"Hey Stupid, your cops already talked to everyone."

Head turning slightly, the killer stole a quick peek at the mirror, and winked.

"Go ahead. Ask your questions, you stupid bloodhound."

She reached for the remote lying on the nightstand and turned up the volume to Ozzy Osbourne's *Bloodbath in Paradise*. She again, took a quick glance at her *mirror, mirror on the wall*, as she'd named it, and winked. Foot tapping to the music, she resumed the watch.

Pierce rang the doorbell at Mr. Adler's house and waited, his face expectant. When no one answered, he rang again. After one more try, he gave up, leaving the Adler residence and driving across the street to the Romero house.

"Ha. Won't get any answers there either, buddy."

Thirty-three minutes passed before Pierce finally reemerged from the Romero household, followed by a young man. The two men conferred briefly and shook hands, the young man going back inside as Pierce returned to his car.

Hmm. Wonder what Don Juan told the bloodhound.

Only when Pierce had left the vicinity did she let go of the slat. She then sat at her desk and meticulously penciled the details of her surveillance onto a notebook page.

As the pencil rapidly pressed against the paper, something about this particular gumshoe allowed a pang of worry to creep into an otherwise confident demeanor.

Gotta keep my eye on that one.

13

FERNANDO

Margarita was waiting for him in the foyer when Fernando came back. She looked like she was about to have a nervous breakdown, arms clamped across her chest as she chewed her lip and rocked from side to side.

Concerned, Fernando grabbed her and pulled her into a hug. She began to cry, deep mournful sobs into his chest. "Why... did they have to... murder... Daddy?" she wailed.

Fernando had no answer for her. He held her quietly and stroked her hair, all the while wondering if the dry cleaners would be able to remove mascara stains from his expensive, hand-stitched, *guayabera* shirt.

When she had cried herself out, Fernando released her. "Come on. Let's go sit downstairs and catch up."

"Okay," she sniffled.

"Did you tell the workers to finish in the living room?"

"No. I forgot all about them."

"No problem. I'll tell them. Why don't you wait for me in the family room? I turned on the heat earlier—should be nice and warm by now. I'll be down in a few and you can tell me all about your life in California."

"All right."

Fernando watched his sister go downstairs before rushing into the half-bathroom to see how badly she had ruined his shirt. He locked the door and inspected the *guayabera* in the mirror. As he suspected, the delicate material was streaked with traces of his sister's makeup.

Coño!

He wet and soaped a hand towel and gently scrubbed the shirt, relieved to see the stains disappearing. Smiling, he searched under the sink and found a hair dryer to quickly dry the shirt. When he walked out of the bathroom, the *guayabera* looked good as new.

In the kitchen, he instructed the workers to go back into the living room to finish. "I'll be downstairs in the family room. Please come get me when you're done."

Fernando hurried downstairs to join his sister.

"What kept you?" Margarita asked.

"Oh, I had to explain a few things to the cleaning crew."

He settled himself next to Margarita on the old but comfortable sofa. The sofa and the coffee table were the only pieces of furniture their mother hadn't replaced when she and Felix moved into their new home.

Fernando jumped up almost immediately. "I'll be right back," he said heading for the basement's laundry room. He returned with a handful of paper towels, plopping down next to his sister again. "Here, blow your nose and wipe your face. You look dreadful."

Margarita playfully elbowed him and smiled, taking the paper towels, and doing as instructed. She then balled up the used towels and tossed them on the table. Fernando sadly smiled. If his father had ever caught him doing something like that, he would have yelled for him to pick up his garbage and deposit it where it belonged. Only the princess could get away with that.

"Nando, why did you go outside with that detective?"

asked Margarita, gazing at her brother's handsome face.

"I remembered I had a card in my glove compartment with the name and number of the girl I was with last night. Didn't want the detective to think I was hiding something."

"Oh. He was annoying, wasn't he?"

"He was just doing his job."

"Well, I didn't appreciate him questioning us about Dad," she said, scowling.

"Never mind him. Tell me, how is life treating you in the Eureka State?"

Margarita perked up. "California's great. The climate is perfect. The slower pace takes a little getting used to, coming from New York, but Joey and I just love it there despite the occasional earthquake...and the traffic congestion...oh, and the smog."

They laughed like they were kids again. Fernando was suddenly struck by how much he had missed her.

"Seriously, I'm happy living in California," she said, smiling. "You really should come visit."

"I'm happy for you, really," Fernando smiled back. "You never know, maybe I'll make it out there someday. Tell me about your dance studio."

"Teaching dance is so rewarding, Nando. Investing in that studio is the best thing Joey and I have ever done."

"Guess all those dance lessons paid off, huh?"

"They really did. We even choreograph a lot of the dances we teach our students. We were working on a new piece just a few days ago. We're putting on a show at our community theatre next month."

"Wow, that's great. Show me," said Fernando.

"What, now?"

"Yes now. Show me your new dance."

He didn't have to ask her twice. Margarita jumped off the sofa and began to twist her entire body, leaping gracefully around the floor in a lively modern dance.

Watching his sister, Fernando smiled with pride. He felt suddenly overcome with love for her, as a river of memories washed over him.

He hadn't always felt close to his baby sister. As the only child for six years before Margarita was born, Fernando had once been the apple of his father's eye. Felix had been over-joyed when Fernando was born. After all, isn't it every father's dream to have a son he can mold into his own image?

Fernando had idolized his father in his early years, emulating him in every way. He copied his father's walk, his mannerisms, even his way of speaking.

When his baby sister was born, Felix immediately dubbed her *la Princesa*, doting on her much as he'd doted on his son. Naturally, Fernando was jealous of the competition, blaming Margarita for his father's growing indifference toward him.

Then, a couple of years after Margarita was born, Felix began to spend a lot of time away from home. On those rare occasions when he came home early, Fernando tried every-thing he could think of to get his father to spend some time with him. Nothing he did ever seemed to make a difference— his dad just brushed him aside as always.

You really showed me your true colors at that picnic, didn't you, Dad?

Fernando had been eight years old when his father had taken him along to a company picnic. His mom had stayed home to take care of Margarita, who was sick and running a fever.

Fernando had been thrilled to suddenly have his father all to himself, but it didn't turn out that way.

As soon as they arrived at the picnic, Felix dropped his son off with the other kids waiting for the start of a treasure hunt.

"Stay here and enjoy yourself. I'll be over there," said Felix, pointing to a group of adults gathered around a nearby table.

"But Dad, aren't you going to watch me hunt for treasure?" asked Fernando.

"It hasn't even started yet, Nando. I'll be back. Just wait here."

Fernando watched as his father sidled over to a table where beer was being served.

When they began lining up the kids and handing out maps, Fernando looked over towards the table. He didn't see his father anywhere. Panicking, he left the line to search for Felix.

The park was lined with matching white tents that had been set up for various games and buffet stations. Fernando frantically searched each one but couldn't find his dad. In his eight-year-old mind, Fernando thought he'd been left behind.

He had just finished searching the very last tent, when at last, his heart beating wildly, he spotted his father emerging from a thicket of trees. He was arm in arm with a woman Fernando had never seen before. Felix laughed as he twirled the woman and caught her in his arms.

Fernando gasped, mesmerized by the streak of sunlight gleaming in the woman's red hair. He thought she might be an angel. Captivated, he stared as his father dragged her by the hand and sat her on a bench, posing her for a photo. As soon as he'd snapped the picture, the mysterious woman jumped off the bench and rushed into his arms. She whispered in his ear, kissed him full on the mouth, and skipped away, Felix sprinted off behind her.

Confused and afraid by what he had seen, Fernando ran back to where his father had left him, worried he'd done something wrong.

He couldn't be sure how much time had passed before Felix finally rejoined him, reeking of booze. For the rest of the afternoon, Felix continued to drop his kid off at some event or other and disappear for varying lengths of time. He kept promising he would come back so the two of them could sit down for lunch, but the afternoon wore on with no sign of him. Hungry and miserable, Fernando finally gave up waiting, and sat down to eat alone. He eyed the other children, most of whom sat laughing and showing off their prizes to their parents.

So many years later, Fernando still resented Felix, who had never apologized for leaving him alone that day.

Had he been paying attention at all, Felix would have realized how thoroughly he'd succeeded in molding his son in his image. Fernando dated a lot as a teenager. He never worried. When he got tired of a girl, there were plenty of others to choose from. As far as he could tell, girls liked bad boys better anyway. Fortunately, he had also inherited his mother's kindness.

Fernando had been reading a comic book in the living room one afternoon, when Margarita came home from school. He caught a glimpse of her tear-stained face as she slammed the door and ran straight up to her bedroom locking herself in.

"What's the matter with the princess?" he called to his mother in the kitchen.

"Let her be, Nando. She probably had an argument with a girlfriend. She'll be fine."

Fernando had tried to get back to his reading, but curiosity got the better of him. He had never seen *la princesa* so upset. Tossing the comic book onto the coffee table, he followed his sister upstairs and knocked on her door.

"Margarita, open the door. It's me, Nando."

She had looked surprised to see her brother standing outside her bedroom door.

"What's wrong, Margarita? Why are you crying?"

She just stood there, wordless, tears streaming down her cheeks. Fernando reached out and embraced her, just as he'd done in the foyer a little while ago.

They sat on the bed and he coaxed the story out of her. A bully two grades above her, had called her a dirty *spic* and other vile names. She had been giving her dirty looks and pushing her whenever she passed her in the hallway at school.

Next day, Fernando picked up Margarita from school.

After she pointed the bully out to him, he was shocked to see she had singled out a skinny girl, not much older than his sister, who was eleven at the time. "Jesus, Margarita, you're afraid of *that* girl?" he mocked. Tears sprang to Margarita's eyes, and Fernando quickly apologized. "Don't cry. I'll have a talk with her. Wait here."

The bully, Nancy, was amid a crowd of other girls, talking and bursting into laughter every few seconds. None of them noticed him approach, until he spoke.

"Excuse me, ladies," said Fernando, his eyes on the bully. The girls around her looked back and forth between their friend and the handsome, older boy.

"Yes?" she asked, smiling, and batting her eyes at him.

Fernando leaned in close to her face. "There's a girl standing over by that car. He pointed behind him without turning around. Do you see her?"

Nancy shifted her body to look behind him. Her friends followed suit.

"Yes," she mumbled, suddenly nervous.

"That's my sister. If you *ever* call her a *spic* or any other name again, or threaten her in any way, you'll have to deal with me. Get it?"

The frightened girl could only nod.

Point made, Fernando went back to his sister and opened the car door for her.

Nancy and her posse never bothered Margarita again.

That was the day Fernando realized how much he loved his little sister. From that day forward, he made sure to watch over her, although he occasionally took things too far and made her angry.

He shook himself from his reverie as Margarita finished her dance. Fernando clapped with enthusiasm.

"Did you like it, Nando?" she asked breathlessly.

"It was wonderful, princesa. You're an incredible dancer."
I've missed you.

14

BB'S TAVERN

I arrived at BB's Tavern late in the afternoon. Stepping into the bar, I felt a moment of disorientation as the gloom surrounded me. I paused just inside the door, giving my eyes a moment to adjust, after the glare of sunlight on the snow.

The semi-dark room felt warm and inviting, making one oblivious to the outside world. There was an old-fashioned jukebox loaded with forty-five rpm records instead of compact discs, an original wooden floor, and a refurbished wooden bar. The pub's ambiance was one of days gone by. You could almost catch the aroma of the tobacco, bourbon and beer that had permeated these walls throughout the years. I could see why Mr. Romero, who wasn't very friendly, had liked to hang out here.

I made my way over to the bar. Unbuttoning my coat and leaning against the edge, I surveyed the scene while I waited for the bartender. There were three men at the other end of the bar slamming shots and enthusiastically talking sports. A couple at a table by the window were munching on nachos, sipping wine, and having a discreet conversation while gazing into each other's eyes. Another pair was at the pool table racking up for a game.

Sitting alone at a booth towards the back of the bar, sat a woman engrossed in paperwork. I took her to be the owner.

Suddenly, I felt a sneeze coming on. I quickly reached into my pocket for some tissues and caught it just in time. When I straightened up again, all eyes were on me. The lovey-dovey couple offered their blessings. I nodded my thanks, feeling a little embarrassed. I have a very loud sneeze.

A man waiting his turn at the pool table, walked over to the jukebox and inserted a coin. I watched as the arm grabbed a record from the spindle and laid it flat, the needle lowering to meet its edge. One of my favorite songs streamed out of the speakers, *Forever and For Always* by Shania Twain. I sang along with the lyrics in my head.

The bartender finished serving her customers and came right over, wearing a friendly smile. "Hi. What can I get you?"

I shut off the music in my mind and pulled my identification from the inside pocket of my overcoat. "I'm Detective Pierce," I said, offering my ID. "I'd like to speak to the owner, please."

The three sports fans at the bar turned their attention toward us, their conversation suddenly hushing. They quickly averted their eyes and went back to munching on their sandwiches when I glanced back at them.

The bartender took my ID, barely looking at it, before handing it back to me.

"She's busy at the moment, but perhaps I can help you," she offered.

"Perhaps you can," I said, slipping my identification back into my pocket. "It's about a customer of yours."

"Which customer?"

"Mr. Felix Romero."

"Oh, him," she scowled. "Yeah, he comes in regularly. Sits

over there at that table in the corner," she said, pointing to the back of the bar. "Orders beer and sometimes nachos."

The table she'd pointed out, was situated a few feet away from the pool table, and a little ways apart from the other tables, probably to make sure people had enough room to play.

"Anyone ever come in with him?"

"Nah, he's a loner. If anyone ever tries to talk to him, he either ignores them, or tells them to get lost. The regulars all know to let him be."

"Has he ever caused any trouble?"

"Not on my shift, but I heard he got into a fight last week and was thrown out. We don't get a lot of fights in here. It's a neighborhood bar, you know?"

"Sure."

"Did he kill someone?"

"Why do you ask?"

She took a moment before answering, "I don't know. Seems like the type, I guess," she shrugged.

"How do you mean?"

She blushed, perhaps regretting her assumption.

"You know, the quiet, loner type," she said, lowering her voice. "He always looks so angry. He gives me the creeps."

"To answer your question, Mr. Romero did not commit a crime. He was the victim of one."

"Oh, no. Did he get mugged or something?"

"Fraid not. He was the victim of a homicide."

"What? Homicide?" she gasped.

I glanced past her shoulder at the men at the end of the bar. The three of them were now shamelessly listening to our conversation, their hot roast beef sandwiches and fries cooling on their plates. I ignored them.

"I'm afraid so."

"Jesus. No one's safe anymore. What happened?" she asked, her eyes wide and frightened.

"I can't give you any more details. This is an ongoing investigation."

"Oh yes, of course."

"Is there anything else you can tell me about Mr. Romero?"

She shook her head. "No, nothing else comes to mind."

"Thank you, Miss…?"

"It's Sam."

"Sam. You've been very helpful. Would you get the owner for me, please?"

Instead of leaving her post, Sam yelled across the room, "BB, would you please come over here for a minute?"

The whole room was looking at us now.

The owner recognized a law enforcement officer waited to speak with her. She had been around police all her life—her father, uncle, and two cousins, were all police officers. She could tell who was who at a glance. She stood and walked over to the bar, a tall, and sturdy-looking woman, with a no-nonsense aura about her. She looked to be in her forties, maybe?

"What can I do for you?"

She had a warm and inviting smile, but at the same time, her eyes let you know who was in charge. Confidence, that's what I got from her.

Whipping out my ID once again, I introduced myself. One of the men at the end of the bar was still watching us. He lowered his gaze when I met his eyes.

After scrutinizing my credentials, she gave the ID back to me. "Please sit, Detective."

We sat at the bar stools. "Would you like a beer?"

"No, thanks. I'm on duty."

"Of course. What can I do for you, Detective?"

"I understand Mr. Felix Romero has been a regular at your establishment."

"Yeah, he came here two or three times a week, until I threw him out recently."

"When was that?"

"Last Friday evening, just before the snowstorm."

"The same evening as the fight? Sam here told me Mr. Romero got into an altercation."

"Yes."

"Tell me about it."

"That guy has never been nice to my staff, grunting when they serve his beer, and never tipping. If someone tries to strike up a conversation, he tells them to leave him alone. That's all well and good, but sometimes he stays too long and gets into other people's business, which invariably leads to an argument. On the night of the fight, he came in and went straight to the back to sit at his usual table, but it was occupied. He grabbed a seat at another table and stared daggers at the men sitting where he wanted to be. Good thing those men were absorbed in their own conversation and didn't notice him then, or else the fight would have broken out much sooner. I guess Mr. Romero was feeling combative."

"How so?"

"For starters, he ordered a third beer, knowing full well two is his limit. Fool can't hold his liquor," she said, shaking her head in disdain. "He got super mopey when I refused to serve him another one, and that's when the shit hit the fan. He suddenly screamed, 'You fucking assholes, that's my table.' Next thing I know, he gets up and throws his empty beer bottle at the people at his usual table. Before you could say, 'Oh shit,' the other guys were pounding him into the floor, all the while he was lashing out in all directions and cursing at the top of his lungs. Scared the crap out of everyone in here."

"Sounds like he was itching for a fight."

"Yeah, you could say that. I had noticed he was brooding that night, so I was keeping my eye on him just in case things got out of hand, but wouldn't you know it? I turned around for one minute to answer a question for one of my kitchen staff, and in a split second, those guys were on him. It happened that fast."

Sam joined the conversation just as her boss finished describing the incident. "He'd almost gotten his ass kicked more than once before that night. Then, he finally got his ass kicked," she laughed.

BB turned to her, annoyed. "Sam, would you please check the kitchen for that pastrami? Table five has been waiting for more than fifteen minutes, and you know how he hates waiting for his sandwich."

"Sure thing, boss," Sam replied, seemingly oblivious to her boss's irritation. She smiled and disappeared into the kitchen.

"How many people were involved in the fight?" I asked.

"There were four of them sitting at the table where that jerk thought he should be, and they all joined the fight. It took both my bartenders, my kitchen staff, and me to get them off of him."

"Anybody hurt?"

She scoffed. "No, but I bet that fool was in a heap of pain the next day. He took quite the beating. As for the others, the bottle didn't even make it close to their table. He had absolutely no coordination."

"Did you file a police report?"

"Nah. No one was hurt, and things settled down again after I threw him out, so I figured, why bother?"

"Do you happen to know the names of the men in the brawl?"

"I know one of them, Rick Bradshaw. Comes here once or twice a week."

"Know where he lives?"

"Only that he lives in Bartonsville."

Out of the corner of my eye, I saw Sam come out of the kitchen carrying a tray.

"Did Mr. Romero attempt to come back after that?"

"Haven't seen him since. If he came by during the storm, I was closed. I made it clear I meant business when I told him I didn't want to see him in here anymore. Warned him I'd call the police if he ever showed up again."

"Anything else you can tell me about Mr. Romero?"

"There's nothing more to tell. Only reason I know his name is cause I overheard him introduce himself to one of my customers when he first started coming here. He was trying to flirt, all gentlemanly-like. She wasn't interested to say the least, so he dropped his gentlemanly manners and insulted her. He accused her of being a lesbo and looking ugly in her nurse's uniform. Typical," she smirked.

"Do you happen to have her name and address?"

"I don't have her address, but her name is Abby Gonzalez. She usually comes by in the evenings after working at Pocono Medical, if she isn't working a double. Says she likes the atmosphere and comes in to decompress. Orders a sandwich and a club soda with a twist. She's been doing that for well over a year now."

"Got it. Thank you for the information."

I took a card from my pocket and handed it to her. "Here's my card. Would you please call me next time Miss Gonzalez, Mr. Bradshaw, or any of his friends come in?"

She took the card and slipped it into her shirt pocket without looking at it. "Of course, Detective. So, what did he do?"

"Mr. Romero was murdered yesterday morning."

Her eyebrows lifted in a moment of shock.

"Well, can't say I'm surprised," she said recovering quickly. "Still, it's terrible to hear he was murdered."

"Thank you again for the information, Miss?"

"It's Bridget, Bridget Bell, but call me BB."

"Thank you BB. It was very nice meeting you."

"Same here, Detective."

Pulling away from the curb, I felt like I had formed a fairly good picture of the kind of man Felix Romero had been.

I had one more stop to make before I could go home to a hot cup of lemon tea and a warm bed.

15

LEGWORK

Outside Mariano's Pizzeria, Detective Ramirez watched as a middle-aged man gingerly carried a stack of boxes down the snow-covered side stairs of the building. He wasn't quite dressed for the weather, wearing only a light jacket over a hoodie, but he did have on snow boots.

"Whoa!" he shrieked as his foot slipped off a step.

Witnessing the spectacle, the detective was impressed with the man's agility. He had managed to grab the handrail with one hand, while keeping the boxes balanced with the other. He made it safely to the bottom of the stairs without dropping a single one. He fumbled with a set of keys, and finally unlocked the door to the pizzeria.

That's gotta be the owner.

Ramirez turned the ignition off and stepped out of his heated car, instantly regretting getting out of bed that morning.

Man it's cold!

He locked his car and headed across the street and into the shop. A bell rang in the back of the store.

"Felix?" hollered an unseen voice.

"It's Detective Ramirez."

"Oh, one moment please."

Anthony Conte rushed into the dining room, with a surprised look on his weathered, but still handsome face. A hard-working, fourth-generation Italian American, Anthony's original vision of life had nothing to do with the one destiny had given him.

Anthony was a native of East Stroudsburg. Upon graduating high school, he had planned on moving to New York City to attend Pace University and study financial management. Like most young people, he wanted to branch out on his own, rather than getting stuck working at the family business just because he was expected to.

Unfortunately for him, not long after receiving his high school diploma, his mother was diagnosed with cancer and died six months later. His parents had known each other since grammar school. When she died, Anthony's father had fallen apart, along with Anthony's dreams.

Unable to function through his grief, the elder Conte died thirteen weeks after his wife's passing. Their only heir, then nineteen-year-old Anthony, inherited the pizzeria and family home. Filled with grief and despair, Anthony had tried to sell the business, without any luck. He had seriously contemplated walking away and letting the bank take it all, but common sense prevailed. He wasn't financially stable enough to let it all go, so he made the best of the situation, and stayed.

Fortunately, working at the shop part time after school and on weekends, had prepared Anthony to run Mariano's. He was grateful for the business education his father had given him, and he worked hard to keep the business from going under. Nevertheless, he still hoped to be able to sell in a year or two—plenty of time to go to New York.

That day never came. A few years later, he got married, moved his wife into the family home above the shop, and accepted his fate.

"I was just about to unpack some new menus. How can I help you, Detective?"

"I'd like to ask you a few questions about an employee of yours, Mr. Felix Romero."

Ramirez flipped opened his ID as the owner approached. Anthony took a quick look and nodded.

"Felix?" he questioned, his brow furrowed.

"Please sit, Detective," he said, gesturing to a nearby table.

Mr. Conte took a seat across from Ramirez. He looked nervous, as people often do when visited by law enforcement.

What is this about? he wondered, sitting straight-backed with clasped hands resting on top of the red and green checkered tablecloth.

Ramirez took a pad and pen from his breast pocket, laying the pad open on the table.

Mr. Conte suddenly remembered his manners. "Can I offer you some coffee? It won't take me long to brew a pot," he said, pushing back his chair and standing.

"No, thank you. I don't drink coffee or tea, bad for my digestion," he smiled.

Ramirez had always been a big eater and a big coffee and soda drinker. For the past few years he had been suffering from acid reflux. His doctor recommended a nutritionist who helped Ramirez avoid acidic food and drink. Although he sometimes missed his coffee and soda, he hadn't had a bout of acid reflux in months, and he was losing weight.

Anthony also smiled. He sat back down, scooting his chair in again and relaxing slightly.

"I'm afraid I have some bad news concerning Mr. Romero," Ramirez began.

"What's he done?" popped out of Anthony's mouth before he could stop himself.

"What makes you think he did anything?"

"Well, I...I just assumed he's in some kind of trouble," Anthony stammered.

"Why do you assume so?"

"It's just...well, Felix isn't a very pleasant human being. I figured he'd gotten into a fight or something. I mean, why else would a detective be visiting me?"

"Mr. Romero was the victim of a homicide," said Ramirez, watching Mr. Conte carefully.

"What? Homicide? You mean Felix is dead?"

"I'm afraid so."

"But how is this possible?" asked Anthony, his voice shaking. "When I heard the doorbell ring, I was sure it would be Felix, late again."

He shook his head. "Oh my God. What happened?"

"This is an open investigation. I can't say anything further, Mr. Conte."

"Please, call me Tony."

"Tony? You're not Mr. Mariano Conte?"

He shook his head. "No. That was my father. He founded the business. After he passed away I took over the shop."

"I see. How long had Mr. Romero worked for you?"

"He started working here about a year and a half ago."

Ramirez wrote the information in his pad.

"To your knowledge, was he ever involved in a disagreement with any of your customers, or with you?"

"A disagreement? Not as far as I know."

"Anyone you can think of who may have had reason to harm Mr. Romero?"

"I dunno. Felix is always in a bad mood, but he pretty much keeps to himself. I know he doesn't...ah...didn't like working here and always talked about his fancy job in the city, but he was lucky I hired him. He should've been grateful for the opportunity. Lots of people out of work right now, you know?"

"Sure. So, Felix and you never argued in the year and a half he worked for you?"

"Wait a minute," he protested. "You're not implying I had anything to do with his murder, are you?"

"Just trying to get the full picture here."

"Look, Felix did a good job for me, although he had a habit of coming in late," Anthony explained nervously. "He'd mumble under his breath and sometimes shoot me dirty looks when I reminded him of his working hours, but he never gave me any back talk. He knew I wouldn't tolerate that. That's as far as it went with our relationship."

"Did he have any friends or acquaintances meet him here at any time?"

"Not that I'm aware of. I really didn't know much about Felix. Trying to start a friendly conversation with him was a waste of time. Only thing I know is, he was married with a couple of grown children. Everything else he kept to himself."

Ramirez made another note in his pad.

"Where were you between the hours of 11 PM Saturday and 8 AM Sunday?"

"What? Are you kidding me? In the middle of a blizzard? I was upstairs where I live, in bed with my wife. Where else would I be?"

"Calm down, Mr. Conte. I'm just doing my job."

"Sorry. This whole thing has really shaken me."

"I understand. Now, may I speak with your wife so she can corroborate you were both in bed on the night in question?"

"All right. Let me give her a call. Excuse Me."

Conte got up and went over to the telephone on the wall. He dialed his home.

"Jen, there's a detective here asking questions about Felix. Would you please come down? No, I don't know. Please, just come down." He hung up and again sat across from Ramirez.

"While we're waiting, may I ask what size boots you wear?"

The question surprised Anthony, but at this point, he figured it was all part of the investigation. "Size eight and a half," he timidly answered, hoping his boot size had nothing to do with the murder.

Although Mr. Conte stood about five feet ten-inches tall, he had small feet for his height. His size eight and a half boots were too small to compare to the shoe pix taken at the crime scene.

Back in his car, Ramirez went over his interview with Mr. and Mrs. Conte. Everything seemed straightforward. No hairs standing at the back of his neck, no hinky feelings.

———

CELIA BYRNE JOINED the team six years ago. Though she was the only female in the group, she nevertheless felt at home among her male colleagues. She was used to being surrounded by an excessive amount of testosterone—almost every man in her family was in law enforcement. Her teammates learned very quickly Celia gave as good as she got. Her quick wit, easy manner, and mathematical abilities impressed everyone she came into contact with.

A natural problem solver with a good head for numbers, she passed the tests to become a homicide detective after only four years as a police officer. Her perfect arrest record proved to be in her favor when she interviewed for the detective's spot.

Analyzing the Romero investments on her computer, she soon had a picture of the couple's debits and credits.

While Mr. Romero had been working as a banker, he and his wife lived very well. Their credit card debt was under control, and they had a nice nest egg in the bank. Their savings and severance pay depleted quickly once the bank let Felix go. Such a normal looking portfolio didn't raise any suspicions for the meticulous Celia Byrne, but she had been fooled before.

She spent the day digging deeper into their financial records, looking for anything out of the ordinary. As daylight faded into evening she finally concluded, like many Americans in their shoes, the Romeros were barely scraping by. Borrowing from Peter to pay Paul had been their way of life for many months by then. If Felix Romero had any extra money hidden away, he didn't seem to be spending it. Celia continued to dig deeper, just in case.

16

LOWELL ADLER

After leaving BB's Tavern, I decided to try Romero's neighbor one more time. If I wrapped this up today, I'd be more prepared for the meeting with my guys tomorrow.

The door opened on the second ring. A man with wet hair and a towel wrapped around his neck, stood before me in running clothes and socks.

"Good evening. Mr. Lowell Adler?"

"Yes?" he cautiously answered.

"I'm Detective Howard Pierce," I said, flashing my ID. "May I come in?"

"Please. It's cold out there."

"Thank you."

"You're welcome. Let me have your coat," he said.

"The living room's straight ahead. Make yourself comfortable. I'll be right over," he said, taking my coat and walking over to the closet in the hall.

I waited for him just inside his cozy living room, taking in the warmth of the burning wood as it crackled in the stone fireplace.

"May I get you something to drink? Coffee?" he asked, poking his head in the door.

"I'd love a cup. Thank you."

"No problem. I'll brew some fresh."

I gazed after him as he walked out of the room with purpose, and envied his thin, muscular body. A middle-aged man whose physique made you suck in your gut when he looked at you.

I made use of his absence to survey the room, taking note of the tasteful furnishings and plush carpet. I was admiring a painting when he came back.

"Do you like it?" he asked.

"It's interesting," I answered noncommittally.

"It's a copy of a famous Matisse, called *Harmony in Red*."

"It's very nice," I answered, knowing nothing about art.

"Please sit, Detective. Coffee will be ready in a few minutes. I'm just gonna run upstairs and put on some dry sweats. I don't want to sit on the sofa in these sweaty clothes."

"Yes, certainly." I sat on the small sofa and pulled out my notepad.

I'd barely had time to go over my notes when he came back and sat down across from me.

"Now, how may I help you, Detective?"

"I'm sure you've heard by now of the homicide at the Romero residence across the street?"

"Of course. It's all over the news."

"Were you at work on Sunday?"

"Yes. I work at Pocono Medical."

"May I ask what you do?"

"I'm a respiratory therapist."

"At what time did you start work on Sunday, and when did you finish your shift?"

"I worked from seven AM until seven PM."

"Long day," I commented, eyebrows raised.

"For sure. I've been working extra hours filling in for a

therapist who's out sick with pneumonia. I've been splitting her shift with another colleague since before the blizzard began."

I wrote this information in my notebook.

"Do you normally begin work at that time?"

"No. My usual shift begins at eight and ends at four-thirty, unless I work overtime, which is rare. Like I said, they've been short-handed at the hospital."

"I see. What time did you get up to get ready for work on Sunday morning?"

"I was up at a quarter to six."

"Did you hear or see any commotion going on across the street?"

"No, of course not. I showered, got dressed, made myself a light breakfast, shoveled the driveway, and left for work."

"Why do you say, of course not?"

"Well, there's no way I would have heard anything. The wind was so loud, and I'm not in the habit of spying on my neighbors."

Bit of an attitude.

"Do you normally go running in the mornings, or evenings?"

"Depends on the day. As you saw, I still had my running clothes on, from the run I finished about five minutes before you knocked on my door."

"Pretty messy out there. How did you manage on those slushy sidewalks?"

"I didn't. I have a treadmill in the basement where I run when the weather's bad. I prefer to run outdoors though. Can't beat the fresh air."

"I see. Did you work your normal hours yesterday and today?"

"Sunday and yesterday I worked the twelve-hour shifts. Today I worked my normal shift."

"Did you come straight home after work today?"

"No. I stopped at the supermarket and the bakery for a few things, before heading home. Why do you need to know this?"

"Nothing to be concerned about. I'm just getting a feel for the neighborhood. Tell me, how well did you know Mr. Romero?"

"Not well at all."

"Why is that?"

"I've only been living here for about three months now, and I really don't have the time to be neighborly."

"Where were you living before?"

"The East Village in New York City. It's a short commute from there to Bellevue Hospital where I was working at the time."

"What made you decide to move here to the Poconos?"

"I was born in Pennsylvania. My parents divorced when I was young, and my mother and I moved to New York City. I used to visit my father in Snydersville every other weekend. It's not too far from here. He died a couple of years ago and I'd been missing coming out here, so when I got tired of city life, I decided to move back."

"I see. Where is your dog, by the way?"

"My dog?" he asked, surprised. "He's in his cage in the kitchen. I put him in the cage whenever I have company, so he doesn't bother anyone."

"What kind of dog is he?"

"He's a miniature schnauzer. He gets rambunctious," he explained, correctly interpreting my puzzled look.

"Terriers are temperamental if you don't understand them, and some people just don't like them. How do you know about my dog, anyway?"

"Mrs. Romero mentioned her husband argued with you, on more than one occasion, about your dog doing his business on their property."

"That man," said Adler, rolling his eyes and shaking his head. "He was always so nasty to me."

"Is it true your dog likes to relieve himself on the Romero property?" I asked.

"I've certainly never seen Chauncey go over there. It's across the street after all, and my dog is afraid of cars."

"Don't you walk him on a leash, Mr. Adler?"

"I do walk him on a leash, yes, but sometimes I just let him out and he comes back. Later, I pick up. After all it's my property he's going on."

"Do you watch him when you let him out?"

"Not every time, no."

"Then how can you be sure he doesn't cross the street?"

"I know my dog," he answered with certainty.

"Okay, let's move on. Tell me about the arguments between you and Mr. Romero."

A beep sounded in the kitchen.

"Excuse me, coffee's done. How do you like yours?"

"Black is fine."

He got up and went into the kitchen.

I took advantage of his absence and walked over to the mat near the front door where I'd noticed a pair of boots when I first came in.

They looked to be about a size ten or so, I guessed, picking them up and examining the pattern of the soles. There was no glass embedded in them as far as I could see. I looked inside for the size and confirmed them to be tens.

I opened the closet door next, and quickly examined the label on the inside of a long coat. The label read, *Insulated with one hundred percent Goose Down Feathers.* There were no obvious tears I could see.

I closed the door again and went back to the living room, managing to get back in my chair just before Adler walked into the room, carrying a tray with two mugs of coffee and a dish full of cookies.

"I bought these on my way home today. Couldn't resist. Please, help yourself."

"Thank you," I said, reaching for my coffee and breathing in the delicious aroma. I blew on the surface of the coffee and tentatively brought the mug to my lips. The taste was like nothing I was used to.

"This coffee is wonderful," I praised.

"Thank you. I buy the beans whole and grind them myself. It's the only way to brew a decent cup of coffee," he boasted.

I could see what he meant. Perhaps I'd surprise Louise with a coffee grinder.

"Please, try a red velvet, chocolate chip cookie."

"If you insist," I said, reaching for a cookie and taking a bite. As cookies go, this one was really good, moist on the inside and crunchy on the outside.

"Good, right?"

"Very good," I agreed.

"They're from the Rufescent Confectionary. Have you been?"

"I'm familiar," I answered. *I guess everyone around here knows that bakery.*

Anxious to get on with the interview, I finished the cookie in one big bite and washed it down with another sip of coffee.

"Mr. Adler. I'd like you to tell me about your encounters with Mr. Romero, please."

He ran his fingers through his damp hair combing back a strand that had fallen over his eye.

"Well, for one thing, I'm not sure why he assumed Chauncey's been the one littering his property. There are plenty of other dogs in this neighborhood. I tried to tell him that, but he just insisted he'd seen Chauncey peeing and pooping all over his yard."

"Any other incidents?"

"Since I've been working these double shifts, my neighbor has been kind enough to feed and walk my dog. Late Saturday afternoon, she called me at the hospital to tell me there was a crazy man banging on my door, in the middle of the blizzard, screaming at the top of his lungs. Scared the crap out of her. Romero said he was going to kill Chauncey if he caught him at his place again. No way was she going to open the door for him."

"How do you know it was Mr. Romero?"

"Are you kidding? Who else would it be? He's the only one who has ever complained about my dog."

"All right. Did you call the police?"

He shook his head. "No, no."

"Why didn't you?"

He ran his hand through his hair again, his expression thoughtful. "I don't know. I guess I was just stressed out and wanted to forget the whole thing."

"Did he ever threaten you, personally?"

"He did, actually. He saw me on the street one time and accused me of being irresponsible for letting my dog run around without a leash. He got all up in my face and said he would punch me silly if my dog ever pooped on his property again. Left me pretty shaken up. His wife confronted me a couple of days later, as I was getting out of my car. She apologized for her husband's behavior, but then said she also saw my dog pooping on their property. I told her they were both crazy, and I came inside."

"Why didn't you believe Mrs. Romero?"

"Why?" he asked surprised. "I told you. My dog doesn't cross the street."

"All right. Were you home all night on Saturday?"

"Yes."

"Can anyone confirm that?"

"I live alone, Sir, and no one spent the night with me if that's what you're asking," he snapped.

"Just trying to establish everyone's whereabouts at the time of the murder."

"Sorry. I didn't mean to be snippy."

"I understand. A homicide in the neighborhood puts

everyone on edge. Did you happen to notice anyone or anything suspicious when you left on Sunday morning?"

He shook his head. "No. Nothing."

"I know you're not in the habit of looking across the street, but did you by chance happen to see the Romero's front door ajar when you were shoveling the driveway?"

"I didn't."

"Okay. One more question. Do you own a firearm?"

"Yes. I own a Smith & Wesson M&P Shield. Don't want anyone thinking they can break in here just because I live alone."

"I understand. Do you have a permit?"

"No need. I'm sure you know Pennsylvania doesn't require one for protecting your own home, and I don't take it out of the house. It's just for my protection when I'm at home."

"Do you mind if I examine your weapon?"

"Why? You don't think I killed that son of a bitch, do you?"

"Just ruling things out," I answered, keeping my voice carefully neutral.

"All right. I'll go get it. Excuse me."

I waited until he had gone upstairs before wandering back to the closet, where I took a closer look at the coat. I had a full three minutes to examine it this time, but I still didn't find anything out of the ordinary. I was again back in my seat when Mr. Adler returned.

"Here, Detective." He handed the weapon over.

I inspected the firearm, which was fully loaded with the safety engaged. I wrote the information in my pad and gave it back, warning him to keep the weapon secured at all times.

"Oh, don't you worry about that. I keep the gun in a safe in my bedroom," he assured me, setting the gun on the table.

"Have you taken a gun safety course?"

"Please," he said, rolling his eyes. "My father taught me how to shoot before I was old enough to shave."

I was done here. I finished the last of my coffee, set the mug on the coffee table, and stood.

"Thank you, Mr. Adler for the information, and the delicious refreshments."

I stuffed the pad and pen into my pocket and pulled out a business card.

"Here's my card. If you think of anything else that might help our investigation, please be sure to contact me."

"I hope you catch whoever killed him, Detective," he said, glancing at the card and setting it next to the gun, "although I can't say I'm sorry he's dead. He was a nasty person. Still, I'll feel safer when you catch the killer."

He walked me to the door.

"Have a good evening, Detective Pierce."

"Evening, Mr. Adler."

17

GREGG SIMPLIFIED

I walked into the police station already mentally reviewing the case.

Before bringing the team up to speed, I remembered to look at the topography map of the Romero neighborhood. The map verified there were no roads leading to the house through the miles of state game lands behind the property.

I entered the squad room to address the team.

"Good morning all."

"Morning," they boomed back with enthusiasm. These guys were primed, and eager to sink their teeth into the new murder mystery.

I got down to it.

"Gentlemen, lady, what have you discovered so far? Ramirez?"

Reading from his pad, Detective Ramirez reported.

"Interviewed Mr. Anthony Conte of Mariano's Pizzeria, where Mr. Felix Romero was employed as a delivery driver. Other that Mr. Romero was a disagreeable SOB, who was chronically late for work, I didn't learn much from this interview. I also spoke with Mrs. Conte, who confirmed they were both in bed at the time of the homicide. Although Mr. Conte is five foot ten, his boots are a size eight and a half, too small to match our footprint."

"Any lingering suspicions?"

"Nah, he's not the calm and collected type to pull off a homicide like this. You shoulda seen him trying to juggle boxes while fumbling with the keys to his shop."

"All right, thanks. Byrne?"

"I went through the Romeros' financial records for the last ten years. Mr. Romero made a rather good living while working on Wall Street, and had a decent amount in the bank, but his savings depleted fairly quickly once he lost his job."

"Find anything unusual?"

"Not so far. No withdrawals or deposits indicating criminal activity or a gambling habit, just a man trying to keep up with expenses."

"Conclusions?"

"I doubt he was murdered for money, but you never know what people are hiding. My contacts haven't found anything to connect Mr. Romero with any hidden stash. His money trail is pretty straightforward, mortgage payments, household bills, the usual. But I'll keep working on it in case there's something I missed."

"Thanks Ceci."

"You bet."

"Ramirez, did you get in touch with your aunt?"

"I emailed her a copy of the note yesterday, but her internet has been down all weekend due to a power outage in her area. I drove over to see her early this morning and showed her the note. She immediately recognized the writing as Gregg Simplified, the same kind of shorthand she learned in high school."

"Was she able to interpret it?"

"She thought so, but she wants to study it further. She promised to get back to me today."

"All right."

"Oh, one more thing…"

Ramirez pulled a wrinkled sheet of paper from his pocket. He ironed it out with his palm and began to read.

"Gregg Simplified uses what is called brief forms. For example, a secretary in a doctor's office might hear the word 'medicine' ten times a day. Taking dictation, she would not write the precise shorthand symbol for medicine. She would abbreviate the symbol to take faster dictation, along with longer medical words like psychotherapy."

"Whoa," yelled O'Malley. "That's a big word. Look it up, Iggy. I think you would benefit from some psychotherapy."

The room filled with laughter and jabs at Ramirez.

"May I continue?" Ramirez patiently asked.

"Yes, please. Teach us some more big words."

Ramirez refrained from reacting and took a moment to make sure there weren't any more comments.

"Weee're waaiting," someone whispered.

Unperturbed, Ramirez continued to read. "Only the person who created the personal brief forms would know their meaning." He looked up at me to see if I understood.

"I see," I answered, nodding for him to continue.

He turned the paper over, and read, "If you take dictation one day and wait until the following day to transcribe it, the shorthand gets cold. Dictation is taken fast. You might not remember it all if you wait to transcribe it. That goes double when you're trying to read someone else's dictation," he finished, folding the note and looking up for my reaction.

"Good job Iggy, but I don't think we'll have that problem. There's only a few symbols on the note from the crime scene. Hopefully, your aunt can help us with that. Thanks."

"No problem."

"I understand shorthand is a dying art. Can't be too many people who still remember how to use it. In any case, we should have something on that front soon. In the meantime, the Post-It and relevant information have been entered into the National Crime Information Center database. Let's see if any other crimes using this MO turn up."

"I'm already checking the databases, Sarge," said Ramirez.

"Good. How about Mrs. Romero's place of work? Anyone go there yet?"

Detective Hanley raised his hand. "I went by there yesterday, but it was closed. I swung by again this morning to see if it was open, and lucky for me, the owner was outside shoveling the sidewalk. By the way, did you know beauty salons don't open on Mondays?"

Celia raised her hand. "I did." The crowd howled.

"All right, all right. Why would I know that?"

"Did she say anything of substance, Kyle?" I asked.

"She had nothing but nice things to say about the missus. Said she's hard-working, friendly, never gossips. 'A really nice lady' is how she put it. When I asked if Mr. Romero ever come in, she said she's never seen him. Mrs. Romero takes the Pocono Pony bus to work every day and even when she works late, her husband has never picked her up. Sometimes one of the hairdressers gives her a ride home."

"Thanks, Kyle. Anyone else have anything to add?"

Detective O'Malley spoke up. "None of the neighbors I interviewed ever interacted with the Romeros. They all agreed the missus seemed nice enough, but since she was married to Felix Romero, they avoided contact with the couple."

He flipped open his notebook. "One neighbor, a Miss Lillian Gil, said she went over to welcome them to the neighborhood when they first moved in. Said Mrs. Romero was very pleasant and friendly, even giving her a tour of the house. They were sitting in the kitchen having a cup of tea, when Mr. Romero showed up, a little tipsy, in her words. Mrs. Romero tried to introduce her, but Romero gave her a look that, wait..." He glanced at his book again. "A look that sent chills down her spine. Miss Gil quickly left and never returned. Yup, it's safe to assume, Mr. Felix Romero was one big A-hole."

"Regardless, let's do our duty and solve this homicide. Good work, O'Malley." He nodded and flipped his notebook shut.

"Speaking of neighbors," I said. "I interviewed Mr. Lowell Adler, who lives across the street from the Romeros. He'd had a couple of run-ins with Mr. Romero over his dog. Repeated pretty much what everyone else has said about the deceased."

"Also, Fernando Romero, the victim's son, voluntarily let me inspect his Glock Seventeen. He travels for work and has a permit for it. It's clean. I also inspected Mr. Lowell Adler's Smith & Wesson M&P Shield. His weapon checked out too."

"Probably more than one neighbor owns a gun, Sarge," Leung interjected. "This is Pennsylvania after all."

"True. It'll be difficult to check out gun ownership for family, neighbors and anyone else Mr. Romero had contact with, without a gun registry, but see what you can dig up, will you, Jun?"

"I'll do my best."

"While Mr. Romero's weapon appeared clean, he might have another one stashed somewhere. Same goes for Adler. Run a background check on them both, and while you're at it, go ahead and run a background check on his sister and her husband, Margarita and Joseph Diaz. We don't want any surprises."

"Will do," Leung responded.

"Since we're dealing with an unpopular victim, the question is, was Mr. Romero's nasty attitude enough to get him killed, or is there another reason? Let's find out, folks."

18

THE NOTE

I returned to my office and recited the passage my wife had framed and presented to me when I made detective. It had become a sort of good luck charm when starting an investigation.

Louise had given me the first book by the British author, R. Austin Freeman. He'd written a series of twenty-one books and forty short stories about a fictional detective, who was practicing forensic science in the nineteenth century, well before anyone called it that. That book hooked me. Over the years, I have read the entire series of Freeman's books and some of his short stories. The passage is from *A Message From the Deep Sea* by Dr. John Evelyn Thorndike. I know it by heart.

When it is discovered that a murder has been committed, the scene of that murder should instantly become as the Palace of the Sleeping Beauty. Not a grain of dust should be moved, not a soul should be allowed to approach it, until the scientific observer has seen everything in situ and absolutely undisturbed. No tramplings of excited constables, no rummaging by detectives, no scrambling to and fro of bloodhounds.

•   •   •

RECITING the passage brought images of the deceased to the forefront of my mind. I turned my attention to my computer. Studying the crime scene photos, I tried to detect even the tiniest clue as to who the murderer may have been.

Mr. Romero had been taken down by a blow to the back of the head, hands and feet bound, right arm shot, knees shattered. Finally, he was finished off by a direct shot to the chest. As if that wasn't enough, the killer had also felt it necessary to spit and throw dirt on Mr. Romero's face after he was dead. And why leave a note written in shorthand? Was the killer playing some kind of game? Does he have a need to confess, but doesn't want to make it too easy for us? Is he daring us to catch him, or could the note possibly be a red herring?

This was no ordinary homicide. Mr. Romero's home was broken into by someone with the express purpose of torturing and killing him. That much was clear, which meant our victim had to have known his executioner.

A couple of hours went by without my notice before Detective Hanley barged into my office.

"Hey, Sarge. I'm about to pick up lunch at the deli. Want anything?"

"What's everyone else ordering?"

"Grilled cheese, roast beef and tuna sandwiches. Ceci and Iggy both ordered salads, dressing on the side, of course," he laughed. "Didn't you hear the drama?"

I had learned a long time ago to shut out the noise from that busy room.

"Nope. I wasn't paying attention to you guys."

"So, what can I get you?"

"Just a small bowl of soup for me please, any kind, so long as it's hot." I didn't want to tempt fate and eat something heavy until this cold had completely left my system.

"You got it."

I pulled out my wallet and took out a five. "Here. Now let me get back to work."

He grabbed the money but didn't leave.

I looked up. "Is there something else, Kyle?"

"Know what would go well with our lunch?" he asked, barely managing to keep a straight face. I decided to humor him.

"No, Kyle, I don't."

"I was thinking," he paused, as if he didn't already know how I would respond. "Wouldn't a nice cold beer go great with our lunch?"

"It sure as hell would, but you know the rules, pal."

"So, that would be a no?" he laughed.

"An emphatic no," I said."

"Hey, I tried," he said, shrugging.

"You're very funny today, Kyle. Now get out of here and let me work."

Amused, I returned to the images on my screen and once again found myself transported to the scene of the crime.

Putting myself in the killer's shoes, I imagined scoping out the house, breaking the window, and climbing in. Once inside, I hear a noise or perhaps see the beam of the flashlight.

The house is dark, but I find the perfect spot to hide at the side of the staircase.

Wait a minute.

I slammed my hand on my desk, pushing back my chair, and getting up to pace.

The house was dark, and yet the intruder had found the perfect spot to hide? Did that mean he had been inside the Romero house previously, or had he had enough time to find his way to the stairs before he heard the noise or saw the flashlight beam?

I slipped back into the role of the murderer.

As I lay in wait for whoever is coming down the stairs, I'm ecstatic when I realize it's the very person I seek.

I wait for him to take a step inside the living room, quietly sneak up behind him and strike him on the back of the head. I take out the zip ties from my pocket, or perhaps a backpack, and tie him up. I then drag him further into the living room and leave him by the wall, like a sack of potatoes. Dragging a chair from the dining room and placing it by the stove where its warm, I sit a few feet away from him, waiting for him to regain consciousness so I can torture him. When Mr. Romero comes to, I watch as he squirms in agony. I shoot his arm, duct tape his face, and smash his knees, inflicting more pain.

In total control, I come near him and perhaps take a moment to say some final words, or maybe I just let him stare at my face before I finish him. When it's done, I stand over the body and perform a ritual whose meaning is known only to me. Objective accomplished, I casually walk out, carelessly leaving the house exposed to the elements.

Then what? Was there an accomplice waiting in a getaway car, or was the killer's own car parked nearby? During my walk around the neighborhood, I hadn't found any empty spots where a car might've been sitting. The nearest strip mall is two miles away. It wouldn't be impossible to walk to and from the Romero residence from there, but it was an unlikely choice in the middle of a blizzard. Too bad there are no store security cameras on Main Street, only the ones in the ATM machines.

I popped my head into the squad room. "Would someone please check with the banks on Main Street to see what their ATM security cameras picked up on the night of the murder?"

"I'll get right on that," volunteered Ramirez.

"Thanks."

I felt increasingly convinced the killer must live nearby and walked to the Romero residence. Any car left for more than a few minutes in the heavy snowstorm would rapidly be covered in snow. After the murder, the killer would've had to clean off the windshield and headlights before driving away, risking being seen by someone peeking out a window or coming home late. Yes, it was reasonable to assume the killer walked to the Romero household. But from where?

Who are you, and what did Felix Romero do that was terrible enough for you to risk freezing temperatures, capture, and even death in order to eliminate him? Or are you mentally ill and acted on impulse? Mentally ill or not, I'm going to find you.

I stretched my legs and walked out of my office for a little break.

Detective O'Malley accosted me.

"Howard, I think I've got something."

"What is it?"

"The shoe footprint found at the scene was made by a boot with a very distinctive pattern. On the sole of the boot, there are arrow-like shapes in the middle, with semi-circles and sixteen smaller circles around the sides and heel."

"Whoa, slow down."

"Sorry. Sarge, I think I found what we're looking for."

"Step into my office and tell me all about it," I said.

O'Malley followed me, barely waiting for me to walk around my desk and get into my chair before he started talking.

"I checked the Internet and found a boot that matches this pattern."

From the folder in his hand, he pulled out a picture of the crime scene footprint and a printed picture of the sole of the boot in question.

"Take a look at these. Those sixteen circles were made by rubber studs."

I grabbed the photos and nodded, seeing the similarities.

"I'll check with Dunkelberger's, Snyder Shoes, and the shoe stores at Stroud Mall to see if they carry this particular style boot," he continued, encouraged. "We might be able to get a customer list."

"Good work," I said, handing back the pictures. "You go find that boot."

"Yes, Sir. On it."

I shook my head and smiled as I watched him spring up

and dash out of the office—a man with a mission. Yes, my team was hunting down those pieces of the puzzle.

Hanley returned with our lunch, giving us a little break before diving back into our investigation. I spent a few more hours going over the facts of the case when my phone rang.

"Detective Pierce."

"Detective, this is BB. Just wanted to let you know Abby, the nurse I told you about, is here now."

"Ah yes, thank you. I'll be right over."

I reached into my desk and took a swig of cough medicine before donning my overcoat.

Ramirez stopped me on my way out.

"Howard, I have the transcription from my aunt."

"Great. Leave it on my desk, would you? I'll check it out when I come back."

"Will do."

AT THE TAVERN, Bridget introduced me to an attractive woman, dressed in scrubs. I could see why the lecherous Romero would hit on her.

The interview took only ten minutes. Miss Gonzalez had nothing new to add, other than what the owner had already told me. Mr. Romero ignored her the next time she came in. He didn't even look in her direction, she said, which she appreciated.

"I kept watching him to make sure he wasn't going to come talk to me, but thankfully, he didn't. Made me nervous just being in the same room with him, but I was ready if he tried to make a move."

"What do you mean?"

"I've started carrying a small can of hair spray in my purse just in case he or anyone else messes with me."

Can't say I blamed her.

Two more customers walked in while I was speaking with the nurse. The owner caught my attention and waved me over.

I thanked Miss Gonzalez and walked over to BB.

"Those are two of the men from the fight with Mr. Romero," she said tilting her head in the direction of the newly arrived customers. "I'll introduce you."

I followed her to their table. "Hi, fellas. This is Detective Pierce. He wants to ask you a few questions about the guy who started that fight the other night, if you don't mind."

They stared at me with surprise and apprehension in their eyes. Mr. Bradshaw smiled at BB before turning to me and asking, "How can we help you, Detective?"

It was just as the owner had described. Felix had screamed and thrown a bottle at them, and they reacted by pouncing on him. Both of them agreed he had it coming. Neither of them had met Felix before that night, and they assured me the other men in their party were friends who lived in New Jersey. The four of them had been out celebrating a promotion. I collected their contact information and bid them a good evening.

Not all interviews bear fruit, but you never know until you try.

I circled back to the precinct, curious to see what Ramirez's aunt had deciphered.

Aunt Maddy had neatly typed the translation above the killer's shorthand symbols.

You believed the lies and turned against me. Now I get to break you. Lie in the dirt, traitor.

19

GENDER

I received the first envelope a few days after we were called to the homicide at Birdview Lane, addressed specifically to me at the precinct.

After the forensic team processed the mail, I studied the index card carefully. Presumably sent by the murderer, the scribbles looked like the ones on the note left at the crime scene. The loops looked to be made by a heavy pen pressure, indicating tension or anger. Both notes were also written in red ink.

My first instinct said this person watches too much television. Sending a note to the lead homicide detective investigating the murder is so cliché. Nevertheless, as the investigation dragged on, I periodically received such mail.

Long before that final, revealing envelope reached my desk, my team and I were up to our necks in legwork, research, phone calls, and paperwork.

It took a few weeks for me to receive Mr. Romero's autopsy report. I skipped over the preliminary information and quickly looked over the findings. I wasn't surprised not to find anything different than what I had observed at the postmortem. The ME had already confirmed much of the information in the report during the autopsy.

No identifiable marks on the body. Blood alcohol level 0.65

Consistent with the three bottles of beer observed at the scene.

An ulcer of the duodenum measured 2.54 cm in diameter

No surprise there.

After reading the autopsy findings, I was suddenly impatient to get the other reports. I picked up the phone and called the forensics lab.

"This is Detective Howard Pierce, Stroud Area Regional Police. Anything on the fiber recovered at the Romero crime scene in East Stroudsburg, February sixteenth?"

"One moment, please."

I put the phone on speaker and got out of my seat to pace.

More than a few minutes later, the tech came back on the line. I leaned over my desk to listen.

"Let's see. The sample fiber contained polyimides used by textile manufacturers, as well as traces of DWR, and the type of silicon dioxide found on the glass where the sample was recovered. We also found traces of goose down feathers."

Hmm. Adler has a goose down coat in his closet.

"These findings are indicative of a nylon apparel treated with a durable water repellent, like the kind typically applied to down garments in order to prevent water from penetrating the insula…"

"Anything else?" I interrupted before she finished her sentence. I was getting anxious for something I could use.

"We also did an analysis of the soil sample," she went on, unruffled. "We found the chemicals imidacloprid, thiamethoxam, dinotefuran and clothianidin, all of which are neonicotinoids."

"Insecticides," I said, still hoping she'd give me something tangible.

"Yes, Detective. The type of insecticides used for pesticide-coated seed treatment. Many growers are still using it even though it's been proven to be harmful to bees."

"Did you find anything that could help us identify the perpetrator?"

"Yes, if you give me a minute. I'll get to it."

She'd lost patience with me. I resolved to soften my tone.

"Thank you. I'm sorry to rush you. I'm just anxious for any information that might lead me to the culprit."

"Then you're going to love what I say next."

My ears perked up.

"No traces of blood, skin, or hair were recovered, but we were able to test the sputum that had pooled between the victim's chin and neck. Though it looked possible the victim had merely drooled on himself, the sample indicates the saliva actually came from someone else. Also, the adhesive stuck to Mr. Romero's face and hair had traces of saliva matching the sputum sample."

Bingo!

"Further, the sample contained high levels of androgens which could be a symptom of PCOS or Polycystic Ovary Syndrome, which means it's likely the sample was from a female, age fifty to sixty. We ran the results through the database but were unable to match the sample to any known offender."

I pulled out my chair and dropped into it, intrigued by this finding.

"You said *likely* from a female. Is it even possible for a male to have these results?"

"It is. While men do not have ovaries, they can still develop some of the features of Polycystic Ovary Syndrome. Studies have shown the disease to be a genetic metabolic disorder affecting men as well as women. Brothers and fathers of women with PCOS also tend to have elevated male hormone levels which can lead to aggressive and irritable behavior, and a high sex drive. Other health risk factors include high LDL levels, and heart and liver problems, among other serious illnesses."

"Interesting. Thanks so much. Please fax over your findings."

"Absolutely, Sir. I was just about to fax the report before you called, as a matter of fact."

"I appreciate that. Thank you again," I said, hanging up and mulling over this latest bit of insight.

It's a bit surprising to think a woman would leave such a grisly scene. Women usually don't go in for bloody killings, poison being their most popular method statistically. If this murder had indeed been committed by a female, the way she had incapacitated her victim, smashed in his knees, and finished him off in a most dramatic fashion, says to me this was one pissed-off woman.

In her lust for what? Revenge? She not only spit on the victim, but must have ripped the tape with her teeth, not realizing she'd left us a present, as CSI Seager hoped. That she had spit on the victim is a bonus. That saliva sample would now spearhead the direction of our investigation, a welcome break in the case.

If the killer was between fifty and sixty years of age, she most likely learned stenography in high school. In those days, secretaries were mostly women. Yes, the more I thought about it, the more likely it seemed Romero's killer was a woman. I doubted there were more than a handful of boys who opted to learn stenography in high school.

We had no suspect yet, but we were making progress. Not only had Ramirez's aunt deciphered the note left on the body, but she had gotten good at making sense of the cards I still received on a regular basis, all of which were postmarked from nearby locations.

The mail was dusted for fingerprints, of course, but both the index cards and the envelopes always came back clean. There weren't even any saliva traces on the envelope sealant. Couldn't get lucky all the time.

Drumming my fingers on my desk with one hand, and covering my eyes with the other, I was so deep in thought, I didn't notice Leung standing in front of me until he spoke.

"Howard?" I jumped, startled.

"Sorry to disturb you. I know how you like to block out everything when you're in the zone." I nodded, smiling.

"What have you got for me, Jun?"

He handed me a stack of papers still warm from the fax. "Ballistics."

"Thanks," I said, skimming over the top page.

"No problem." He left me to read the report.

The document confirmed the trajectory of the two nine millimeter bullets. The first had been fired from 2.43 feet away by a bolt-action gun, 3.175 inches in diameter, cylinder about twelve inches long. The kill shot had been at point blank range.

I was disappointed to learn the bullets were not micro stamped. Between that and the striations of the cartridge cases, it would be difficult to precisely identify the weapon.

Now that it was suspected the culprit was female, the paperwork piled up before me took on an entirely different meaning. Considering the recent information, I redefined the killer's profile.

A quick search of the NCIC database, produced a homicide case from New York City in the 1960s matching my criteria. In that investigation, a similar note had been left at the crime scene, also in shorthand. The lead investigator on the case, a Detective Fred Jones, had retired ten years earlier and still lived in the city. I managed to track him down, and he graciously agreed to meet with me that very afternoon.

My case file was getting fatter by the week.

I was just getting ready to leave when my phone rang. It was Fernando Romero.

"Yes, Mr. Romero?"

"I had a long talk with my mother, Detective. She told me some things that might be of interest to you."

"I'm listening."

"I was hoping to come to your office to discuss it."

"I don't have the time at the moment. I was just on my way out. I'll be back tomorrow if you'd like to come in then."

"Well, I guess it can wait until then. Mind if I drop by tomorrow afternoon?"

"All right, let's say four o'clock tomorrow at the precinct, 100 Dey Street."

"That's perfect. See you then."

"Goodbye."

I turned off my computer, put on my coat, and walked out of my office.

"On my way to New York fellas," I announced to the squad room at large. "You're in charge, Corporal Ramirez."

20

DETECTIVE JONES

Traffic on the way to the city flowed smoothly all the way up to the Holland Tunnel. It was a good thing I'd left after the morning commuter crowd. Coming back, on the other hand, was going to be a bitch if I couldn't get out again before the evening rush.

Exiting the tunnel into lower Manhattan, I headed north towards the West Village and promptly got lost in one of the few parts of the city that isn't laid out neatly on a grid. Only after being honked at numerous times and yelled at by a particularly angry pedestrian, was I able to get my bearings again.

No matter what time of the day or night it is, the streets in the city that never sleeps, are always jammed with too much traffic and too little parking spaces. Add lost tourists and New Yorkers who pay little attention to traffic lights to the mix, and the experience can be quite harrowing.

By the time I turned on Detective Jones' street, I had made the decision never to drive in this town again.

I had been worried I wouldn't be able to find parking nearby, but lucky for me, a car pulled away from the curb before I reached the corner. It was a tight spot, but I managed to wiggle my car in without too much hassle.

Grateful to be out of the car, I took an extra few minutes to stretch my legs and admire the architecture of the buildings along Jane Street.

Detective Jones lived in one of those lovely tri-level brick townhouses — the kind I will never be able to afford. Stairs led up to the front door and down to the right of the building. At the bottom of the stairs was a gated patio with a cement bench and table, surrounded by various potted plants whose flowers were just beginning to bud. On a sunny and warm day, it must be nice to sit out here reading the paper with a cup of coffee in your hand.

Looking up and down the rows of quaint townhomes, I wondered how on earth a homicide detective could afford to retire in such an expensive-looking neighborhood.

I climbed the stoop and was about to knock when the door opened before me.

"You must be Detective Pierce."

Standing before me was a broad-shouldered, six-foot-three, African American male. His clean-shaven face accentuated his wide, friendly smile, the kind of smile that brightened his whole face and made him look years younger, despite his silver hair.

"I am," I answered, extending a hand."

"I'm Fred Jones," he said, his grip powerful as we shook hands. "And before you say it, not the Scooby Doo character," he said, his smile broadening. "Nice to meet you, Detective."

"Scooby Doo? Aren't you Fred Jones who played for the Kansas City Chiefs?" I teased.

Jones let out the loudest laugh I had ever heard. He practically choked on the words, 'Good comeback.'

"It's Fred, please. Come on in."

A woman in an apron appeared in the hall as I stepped inside, bringing with her the tantalizing aroma of home cooking. My stomach gurgled inaudibly, I hoped.

Jones brightened. "Detective, this is my wife, Sophia."

You know that feeling you get when you see two people together and immediately know they're connected? That's the feeling I got when Mrs. Jones stood next to her husband, who towered over her. Jones beamed, wrapping an arm around her waist.

"It's a pleasure to meet you," she said, extending her delicate, manicured hand.

"The pleasure is mine, Mrs. Jones."

"Please, call me Sofia. Come in and make yourself comfortable," she said, leading the way to the living room.

I felt like I had walked onto a movie set. The room was sumptuously decorated with gorgeous landscape paintings and a massive antique rug. I couldn't help but stare at the beautiful fireplace, set into the exposed brick wall towards the back of the building.

After making sure I was settled comfortably, on what looked to be an antique leather couch, Mrs. Jones disappeared for a minute and returned with a carafe of hot coffee. She made me promise to stay for lunch before excusing herself, and returning to the kitchen, leaving her husband and I to talk business.

Detective Jones got right down to the matter at hand.

"I pulled out my file on the murder of Jessica Mont, right after you called," he said.

He reached for a fat manila envelope on the coffee table. "Here, I made these photocopies for you to take back."

"Much appreciated," I said, setting the heavy envelope in my lap.

"No problem at all," he said, sliding a tattered file towards him and pulling a well-worn pair of spectacles from his shirt pocket. "From what you told me on the phone, it seems our cases share certain pertinent similarities indicative of repeat offender." He adjusted his reading glasses and opened the file.

"Like what?" I asked, curiosity piqued.

"Well, for one thing, the message found at your crime scene

shares certain similarities with the torn piece of stationery left on the body in my investigation."

"You don't say?"

"Absolutely. This particular piece of paper was the fancy type women used to send to friends in that flowery handwriting, back when letter writing was still an art."

"I remember. People don't write letters much anymore."

"Pity. Nothing like getting a hand-written letter from a loved one."

"I absolutely agree. Any fingerprints on the note?"

"Yes indeed. There were fingerprints of both the deceased and her niece, who quickly became my number one suspect. When I asked her why her fingerprints were on her aunt's notepaper, she said her aunt had arthritis, and she often wrote letters for her."

"Ours was clean," I said.

"Well, a lot of good those fingerprints did us."

Jones pulled a sheet of paper from his file and passed it across the coffee table. "Here's a copy of the message and its transcription."

I felt a familiar stirring in my gut as I read. Perhaps this new information would finally bring me closer to solving my case.

"The writing on our note was identified as Gregg Simplified shorthand. Yours looks similar," I said.

"Yes, we also verified Gregg Simplified. This was back in 1966 when shorthand was still part of a commercial course in high schools. We spoke with a Mrs. Alice Martini, one of the teachers at Charles Evans Hughes High over on Eighteenth Street. She verified Gregg and transcribed the note for us."

He glanced at the note for a second before flipping it over and reading the transcription.

"Like my pencil eraser I erase you. Sleep in the dirt where you belong. Goodbye you witch."

"Sounds contemptuous."

"That it does."

"Did you find any other notes of a similar nature in the suspect's household?"

"No, just a bunch of shorthand steno pads filled with symbols, all confirmed as homework by Mrs. Martini."

Just then, Mrs. Jones stuck her head out of the kitchen.

"Lunch will be ready in thirty minutes, gentlemen."

"Thanks, Soph. Smells wonderful," Jones replied with a smile.

He turned his attention back to me. "Mrs. Martini also explained, Gregg gives you the ability to make up your own personal shorthand symbols. She told us while it's not advisable to overuse those personal symbols, it's an acceptable method if the same words or phrases are repeated enough times."

"I'm aware. Brief forms were also explained to me."

"Okay, good. According to Mrs. Martini, the note from our crime scene was easy to decipher. She said all of the symbols used were basic phonetic strokes. Based on that, she thought it safe to assume the note had been written by a student who wasn't comfortable enough yet to create personal shortcuts." I nodded, intrigued.

"Can you give me a little more background on the case?" I asked, taking another sip of coffee."

"Sure thing. There should also be a page in that envelope outlining the pertinent facts," he said. I eased the fat stack of papers out of the envelope and found the outline right on top.

"Wow, thank you. You didn't have to do that," I said, both surprised and grateful.

"It's no trouble. Makes me happy to dive into this case again."

I understood that sentiment perfectly well and smiled as I looked over the outline.

"The victim was one Jessica Mont, maiden name Gil, Female, Caucasian, age fifty-nine. Married Gregory Mont in

1943, widowed in 1944. Her husband was killed in action in World War II," he explained. "They had no children."

Jones picked up the carafe and poured himself another cup, gulping half of it down in one go. Referencing his notes again, he continued.

"The victim's relative, Anna Mont, was residing with her at the time of the murder. Mrs. Mont had taken in her niece after the girl's mother died in 1958. Jessica Mont was killed in her bed by a nine-millimeter bullet to the chest fired at close range. Ballistics determined the class characteristics matched a bolt-action gun, possibly with a suppressor. None of the neighbors we spoke to heard the shot."

"We never recovered the weapon. At that time, there were no gun registry laws in New York City. With no murder weapon and no witnesses, we didn't have a whole lot of avenues to explore."

"Did you have any suspects other than the niece?"

"No. She was our primary and only suspect."

"Immediately?"

"Mm hmm. For one thing, the body was discovered by said niece," he said. There was no sign of forced entry, and the niece was taking a commercial course at Charles Evans Hughes High School at the time, that included Gregg Simplified shorthand."

"Makes sense."

"We searched the house, of course, but we didn't find any incriminating evidence. We even searched her locker at school and the bakery where she worked. All the pieces fit, but we couldn't make it stick. And to add insult to injury, my number one suspect had an alibi. On the morning of the murder, Anna Mont was at her aunt's bakeshop, where she worked part time. More coffee?"

"I'm good, thank you," I said, shaking my head.

He set down his notes, drained the remainder of his coffee and again reached for the carafe. "You'd think I would have broken the too-much-coffee-habit after all these years, but some habits are just too good to give up. Better than smoking at least. I was a smoker for over thirty years and believe me, that habit was a bitch to kick. No way am I gonna give up coffee after that. What's the point of living if you have to give up everything you love?"

He let out a powerful belly laugh.

"I know exactly what you mean," I said. "I still get the urge for a cigarette every once in a while, and it's been years since I quit smoking. My wife had a lot to do with that," I said, remembering how hard it had been for me to kick the habit. "After our first child was born, she kept saying things like, 'You want to live long enough to go to your son's wedding, don't you?' She said that to me once after a particularly long coughing fit, and that's all it took. I quit cold turkey."

"Wow, I'm impressed."

"Don't be. It was the hardest thing I've ever done, but every time I started craving a cigarette, I'd think of that question and forced myself to do something else until the feeling passed. I ate a lot of junk food during those first few months — had to put in some time at the gym, but I did get to attend my son's wedding and my daughter's. Totally worth it," I finished.

"I hear that. My wife is trying to wean me off coffee," he said with a wink.

"By the way" I said, lowering my voice conspiratorially, and trying not to laugh out loud. "I also love my coffee. I try to keep it to five, maybe six cups per day," I joked.

"Amateur!" We laughed like old friends.

"Better get on with this before my wife comes in to get us for lunch," Jones said, setting his cup down and picking up the file again. He flipped to the next page.

"Suspect swore her aunt had been sick the night before and had asked her not to wake her in the morning. She allegedly told Anna to open the shop earlier than usual to get a jump on the weekend orders."

"What time did the other employees get there?"

"Let me see," he said, thumbing through the pages.

I sunk deeper into the big, cozy couch as I waited, fighting the urge to close my eyes and take a nap. I was loving this house more and more by the minute.

"Bakers usually arrived around five AM," said Jones. "Suspect said she was there by four fifteen. When she got home after school, she went to check on her aunt and found the body. The bakery workers all confirmed Anna had been hard at work when they came in at five. They told us she stayed until eight, at which point she left for school. We confirmed her attendance with the school as well."

"Moreover, we discovered no gunpowder residue or splatter on either her clothes or her skin. Of course, she had more than enough time to bathe and discard any incriminating clothing before anyone else showed up to work. We never did find any garments implicating her of the crime."

"What was the time of death?"

"Let's see," he said, looking at the report again. TOD was between midnight and three AM." He took another sip of coffee.

"Distance from the crime scene to the bakery?"

"Three miles. I know what you're thinking. There would have been plenty of time for her to commit the murder and still get to the shop before anyone else showed up. I had the same thought. The girl was in great physical condition—ran track. She could have easily run the three miles."

"How did she say she got to the bakery that morning?"

Paging through the file again, Jones responded, "Said she took the 4:05 bus which picked her up across the street from her apartment and dropped her off on the same block as the bakery. We couldn't dispute her."

"You check the bus schedule?"

"Sure. We confirmed the 4:05 and interviewed the driver on that morning's run. He couldn't say for sure whether or not the girl was on his bus; claimed he didn't normally notice his passengers unless they spoke to him, which was rare."

"Well, your suspicions were certainly credible."

"Credible sure, but nothing we could prove."

"Other than opportunity, were you able to determine a motive?"

"The suspect indicated Mrs. Mont ran a tight ship. She was quite strict, apparently, but Anna didn't consider her to be a bad person. She said she was grateful for everything Mrs. Mont had done for her."

"What about the girl's father? Any information on him?"

"No. As far as we could determine, father unknown."

"Neighbors?"

"Neither the neighbors nor the bakery customers ever witnessed any disagreements between them, though more than one expressed concern the girl was verbally abused. The bakery employees all confirmed the deceased was highly unpleasant and prone to yelling. Apparently, she bossed her niece around just as much as she did every other employee. As a matter of fact, no one we interviewed had anything particularly nice to say about the victim. The stories we heard about her had a similar theme—Jessica Mont was disagreeable and unkind."

"Same as my victim," I said.

Jones shook his head and continued to read. "The body was sitting upright against the pillow, with her mouth open and her eyes wide, indicating she had been awake before she was killed. Whoever was in her bedroom that night had wanted her to know what was happening. One more thing, her face was covered with dirt."

I sat up, immediately on alert. "Let me guess, ordinary potting soil thrown on the victim's face, postmortem?"

Jones peeked over his bi-focals. "Exactly right. Significant to your case?"

"Oh yes. Our victim also had soil thrown on his face after death."

"You don't say?" said Jones, his eyebrows raised. "I'm beginning to think my suspect has done it again."

I was feeling more and more optimistic about that long-ago homicide.

"It certainly seems possible. What else can you tell me?"

He leaned back and pursed his lips. "As I mentioned earlier, our investigation didn't lead to anyone other than the niece. In the end, we couldn't find enough evidence to prove our case," he concluded with a tinge of frustration.

Glancing at the fact sheet, I said, "I see here, you were the one who conducted the interrogation."

"Yes, Sir. Anna was a tough cookie. Acted inconsistent for someone who had just discovered a dead body—overplayed her grief. I tell you, there are some things about this case I've never been able to forget."

"Such as?"

"Like the coldness in her eyes when she spoke about her supposedly dear departed relative. Some things you just can't fake. I know she was the one who did in Jessica Mont."

"She ever send you any letters?"

"Yes, I was just about to look for them. She sent me a few notes before she graduated high school, all written in shorthand."

"Really? I assume you had the notes transcribed?"

"Sure," he answered, rummaging through the file. "There're in here somewhere."

He pulled out a few envelopes. "Here they are."

"Mind if I take a look?"

"Of course not. Take your time."

I eagerly poured over the letters. They were all written in red ink, and the type-written envelopes were post-marked NYC.

"Did the suspect have a typewriter at home?"

"No. We confirmed the envelopes were typed on the same kind of typewriter they used up at the school, but we couldn't narrow in on her with so many students all using the same typewriters."

"Too bad."

"Mrs. Martini transcribed the notes for us, although she couldn't positively say for sure they were written by Miss Mont. The slant of the symbols indicates a left-handed person. There were three left-handed students in her class, but when she showed me their homework, the symbols looked nothing like the ones in my notes."

"Clever girl," I said.

"That she is. Mont is not left-handed and as far as we know, not ambidextrous either. Even so, I'll bet good money she used her left hand to write those messages."

I turned the notes over and read the short translations. Each one was basically insulting his stupidity. I put them into their respective envelopes and passed them back to Jones.

"Did she ever slip up?"

"I kept tabs on her for the next decade, but I never discovered any criminal activity. I know I should have let it go a lot sooner, but I just couldn't do it. You know that feeling you get when *you know* you have the right suspect, but you just can't prove it?"

"Unfortunately, I do."

"In all the years since that homicide, whenever I think about that case, the same feeling returns."

"Were there any other murders that followed a similar pattern during those ten years?"

"We kept her correspondence out of the papers in case similar notes showed up in another homicide. You know how it is."

"Absolutely."

"I kept following up on Anna until my retirement, but to answer your question, no, no other shorthand notes were left at any subsequent homicides. She stopped mocking me after she graduated. Why bother me when she knew she'd gotten away with murder, right?"

I understood and fully sympathized with his frustration.

"Do you miss police work?" I asked, steering the conversation into more neutral territory.

We drifted into banter and swapping stories, common topics whenever law enforcement officers get together. Detective Jones had a way about him that put me at ease. Soon enough, Mrs. Jones called us in to the dining room, where a sumptuous lunch awaited. I hadn't realized how hungry I was until I tasted her incredible stew.

"This is delicious. What kind of soup is this?" I asked as I tore a hunk of fresh baked bread off my dish.

"This is called Bigos stew, made with pork and Polish sausage. You can also make it with venison or rabbit, but I wasn't sure if you liked those," Sophia said.

"I've never eaten rabbit, but I like venison. By the taste of this stew, I'm sure whatever meat you'd prepared this with, it would have tasted just as good."

Sophia bowed her head slightly. "Thank you."

"How long have you lived in this beautiful home?" I asked, wiping my mouth with a cloth napkin.

Mr. and Mrs. Jones looked at one another and smiled.

"Bet you're wondering how we can afford a place like this," Fred teased.

"The thought did cross my mind," I grinned.

"This old house belonged to Sophie's parents. She grew up here. When Sophie and I got married, they moved to Florida and gifted us the house. Believe me, when they bought it back in the 1940s it didn't cost the three mill it's worth today."

I whistled at the figure, causing the couple to laugh heartily.

With my belly full and my head spinning with the new information, I was ready to take my leave.

"Thank you so much for the wonderful lunch, Mrs. Jones."

"It's Sophia, remember? And you're welcome to visit anytime you're in the city, and please bring your wife with you next time."

"I will, Sophia. Thank you."

Jones walked me to the door.

"We certainly have more than a few commonalities in our cases for me to explore," I said as we shook hands. "I'll keep you updated on our progress."

"If your investigation leads to closing my old case, I'm more than happy to cooperate with anything else you need," he said, throwing an arm around me and pulling me in for a hug.

"By the way," I said, pulling away from him, "Do you happen to know what your prime suspect is up to these days?"

"After graduation she worked at the bakery for about seven or eight years before putting the house and business up for sale. Like I said, I kept close tabs on her, hoping she'd give me any reason to arrest her. Unfortunately, she never did. Once she sold both properties, she moved uptown, and that's all I know."

"Okay. We'll talk soon," I said, and hurried down the steps.

21

FERNANDO'S CONVERSATION

J ust as I feared. I hit rush hour traffic on my way back home. Not only did getting through the Holland Tunnel take forever, but once on the highway, the westbound traffic was stop and go. It finally opened up at Exit 19.

How do commuters endure making this trip back and forth all week? I had never been so glad to cross the Delaware Water Gap.

On the bright side, the long ride gave me plenty of time to mull over what I had learned. Jones was right—there were a lot of similarities between our two cases. Both victims had been shot by a bolt-action weapon, likely with a suppressor. In both cases, soil had been thrown on the victim's face after death, and a note was left at the crime scene, written in shorthand. The parallels between the two cases are too many to ignore.

I arrived at the precinct determined to find a connection between Anna Mont and Felix Romero. When I was finally settled at my desk, I devoured the file Detective Jones had so graciously pulled together for me.

I hardly slept at all that night.

I got a call the next afternoon informing me Fernando

Romero waited for me downstairs. I'd forgotten to expect him today.

He was slouched down in a chair in the lobby when I arrived, absorbed in his newspaper.

"I hope I haven't kept you waiting too long, Mr. Romero," I said as I approached. He took a second before tearing himself away from the paper.

"No, not at all," he said, folding his paper and standing for a handshake.

Social formalities over, I escorted him to an empty room where we could talk.

"Please sit," I directed, getting right down to it.

"You said you spoke with your mother?"

"Yes," he answered, settling into his chair.

"I asked her to tell me more about my father. It was like a dam had burst. She couldn't stop talking about his failings as a husband. But the most revealing and significant thing she said, and perhaps the most relevant to you, Detective, was when she admitted she hadn't told you the whole truth when you asked about my father's infidelity."

Just as I'd suspected.

"She told me about a woman my father had an affair with back in New York. He had a hard time getting rid of her once he ended it, apparently."

There it was again, that glimmer of amusement in his eyes and a twitch in the corner of his mouth. Probably waiting for my reaction before attempting a smile.

"Go on," I urged, careful to keep my expression neutral.

"Every so often the phone would ring and if she picked up and said hello, she heard the dial tone. Mom never questioned him about it, and he never offered any explanation."

Fernando leaned towards me. "When I asked her why she hadn't confronted him, she told me she couldn't face the truth. After a few weeks, the calls abruptly stopped. Honestly, I don't know how she put up with it."

"Approximately how long ago was this?"

"Mom said my sister was a toddler at the time, so about twenty-eight, twenty-nine years ago, maybe?"

"Do you know if the other woman ever threatened your mother?"

Rolling up the paper, he sat back and began to gently tap it on his thigh. "I don't think so, but she did call my mom once, when dad was at work."

"Did she tell you what the conversation was about?"

"She didn't give me the details, but she did say she hung up when the woman started describing her affair with my father in lurid detail."

Rubbing it in her face, it sounded like.

"And your mother still didn't confront your father about it?"

Fernando shook his head. "She said she never told my father about that call. Mom cried a lot when she was telling me about it. Believe me, I had a hell of a time trying to comfort her."

"I'm sure it was an uncomfortable conversation to have with her son."

"I know. I felt a little uncomfortable myself."

"Did she tell you anything else about the affair?"

Fernando perked up and stopped tapping.

"I'll say. Apparently my father's mistress sent a package full of Polaroids of the two of them in various, ah... sexual poses, mailed directly to my mother. As you can imagine, it shook her up pretty bad."

"Any chance she kept those photographs?"

"I wish. I mean I wish she'd kept them to help in your investigation," he added hastily, when he noticed the look I was giving him.

"What did she do with the photographs?"

"She said she burned them in the incinerator and never told anyone about them. I couldn't believe she didn't throw them in dad's face. When I asked her why she didn't say anything to dad, she said she got scared and didn't know what to do."

"What's your take on it? Do you think she regrets not confronting him?"

"Look," Romero said, his voice tense. "My father was a womanizer. This woman wasn't the only one he'd cheated with. Even as a kid, I was aware of my father's indiscretions."

"You were?"

"Yes. Whenever we were out anywhere or had people over to the house, all dad needed was a few drinks and off he'd go, flirting with some woman."

"I see."

"Mom said she wasn't fooled by dad's lies. She said she always noticed his staring, and the way he got anxious when he was trying to come up with an excuse to disappear on her. You know how an animal in the zoo paces back and forth inside its cage?"

"Yes."

"That's how he seemed to her whenever he wanted to go after another woman. Mom described my father as a sleep-walker when he followed women. If she ever complained, he'd just deny it and accused her of overreacting. I don't think it ever occurred to him he was hurting her."

Fernando blew out a breath, and said, "I wish she would have thrown those pictures in his face. I think that would have given her a modicum of satisfaction."

"Did the caller leave a name by any chance, or was there an address on the package at all?"

"Nothing on the package, but she did mention her name during the phone call, apparently. Ann, I think — no, Anna."

Unconsciously, I leaned forward.

"Did she give a last name?"

"Just her first name," said Fernando, shaking his head. "Do you have a suspect?"

"A person of interest, perhaps," I answered carefully.

Romero sneered. "Don't tell me that woman followed my dad here. That tryst took place decades ago."

There it was again—that glimmer of mischief and amusement in his eyes, as if he enjoys the fact his father was an adulterer.

I laced my fingers before me, staring Romero in the face. "That I don't know, but I'm sure as hell going to find out. Thank you for the information, Mr. Romero," I said, standing to signal the end of the interview.

He tucked his folded paper under his arm. "Sure thing, Detective. I hope it helps."

We shook hands, each gripping a little harder than strictly necessary. As I watched him walk out, I wondered what was it about all this drama that gave him some weird sort of pleasure?

Later that evening, after I had checked in on Louise, I went into the den and began my search for the Mont family tree. Believe me, it's not as easy as you might think, especially when you don't know a lot of familial connections.

I put the rest of the team to work on the family tree as soon as I got to work the next morning.

It took weeks for us to unravel the complicated family history, but eventually, we hit pay dirt. With that discovery, we finally had a motive.

22

RUFESCENT CONFECTIONERY

I returned to my office to find the telephone ringing. It was Louise, asking me to pick up the cake from the Rufescent Confectionary. She would do it herself, she explained, but she still had a million and one things to do before my birthday party that night.

"No problem," I assured her.

"Thanks, Howie. I owe you one," she said, laughter in her voice. I quietly laughed along at our private joke—I was going to get lucky tonight.

Just as I was about to come back with a sexy remark, Hanley walked in.

"Gotta go now," I said, meaning someone was within earshot.

"All right," she laughed. "Love you."

"Me too," I whispered and hung up.

"What is it, Kyle?" I asked, ignoring his mischievous grin.

"I just brewed a fresh pot of coffee and wondered if you wanted a cup."

"No, thanks, Kyle. Gotta run an errand."

There were three people waiting in front of me at the

Rufescent Confectionary, but for some reason the woman behind the counter called out to me.

"I believe these folks were here first," I answered, gesturing to the people in line ahead of me.

"Were they? I'm sure you'll be quick."

"No really, Ma'am. Please take care of them first."

The woman in front of me turned and whispered, "You'd better go on up. She'll only keep us waiting longer."

"What?"

"May I help you, Sir?" persisted the woman behind the counter.

Doing my best to ignore the pleading eyes from the others in line, I stepped up to the counter.

"I'm here to pick up a cake for Louise Pierce."

"Oh yes, the fifties cake. I'll be right back."

I glanced down at her feet as she went through the swinging door to the kitchen. Yes, everyone is a suspect in a murder investigation as far as I'm concerned.

A baker happened to walk past the kitchen door just as the owner went through. In the brief moment before the door swung shut again, she glanced over and made eye contact with the detective. She dashed out of sight almost as soon as he had seen her.

While I waited, I contemplated the various baked goods in the display case. Every single item, cookies, brownies, cupcakes and more, was embellished with red piping or frosting in one form or another.

Something was nagging me, tickling at the back of my mind, just out of my grasp. What was it? What was I missing?

I was still lost in thought when the owner came back through the door.

"Let's take a look," she said, setting the box on the counter and lifting the lid. "It's a masterpiece, don't you agree?"

Surrounding an intricate jukebox, skillfully adorned forty-five rpm records spelled out the words, *Happy Birthday Howard*.

"Absolutely. This is a work of art, Ma'am."

"It is," she said without a trace of modesty.

"Did you decorate it?"

"I did."

"You do beautiful work."

"Thank you," she said, her eyes glowing with pride. "Your wife already paid for it. I'll just tie it up for you."

"Thank you."

When she was finished, I grabbed the box and made my way out, whispering my apologies to the customers still waiting in line.

BACK IN THE KITCHEN, the baker leaned against the counter, trembling. Her immediate thought upon seeing the detective was that he had come to arrest her. She was relieved when her boss asked her to pass her the birthday cake she had baked earlier, which must have been for him.

She had walked into the bakery a little over seven years ago, looking for a job. Judging by the looks of the place, the owner, Miss Wagner, didn't know the first thing about running a business. Wanting to keep her anonymity, Anna was confident she could come to an agreement with the owner once she showed off what she could do.

She baked a beautiful three-tiered red velvet cake, decorating it with buttercream roses in varying hues of red. After a single bite, Miss Wagner hired her on the spot. She even agreed to pay her under the table, as long as she promised never to mingle with the customers. She was to stay in the kitchen hidden out of sight, churning out beautiful masterpieces while her boss took all the credit. The new hire had just one request in exchange—that the owner would change the name of the bakery. Wagner resisted. She didn't want to give her shop some strange name she didn't understand. She finally gave in when the baker threatened to walk out.

The very talented Anna Mont still had plenty of money from the sale of the house and the business she'd inherited. Much to her surprise, her aunt had also left her quite a sum of money in her will. When she moved to the Poconos, Anna assumed a false identity in the guise of Lillian Gil, not because the police were looking for her, but because the name, 'Mont,' a name she detested, had been forced on her. She'd come upon the name, Lillian Gil, while going through her aunt's belongings after her death. When she moved to the Poconos, she decided that's the name she was going to use in her new life.

Because she didn't have the proper paperwork to apply for a mortgage, she purchased her house in cash. Soon she became bored in what she considered to be a sleepy little town. She missed creating her beautiful confections. Moreover, the cash she kept in her safe at home wasn't going to last forever. The arrangement she made with Miss Wagner suited both parties just fine.

Business at the bakery boomed as Anna, now Lillian, filled the shelves with incredible cakes, cookies, muffins, pastries, and breads, all with the bakery's signature red. Miss Wagner basked in the influx of compliments, even though her customers considered her to be a very rude woman. Relegated to the kitchen, Anna was nevertheless happy to be doing what she loved again. She kept her contempt for the owner quiet, a woman who neither knew nor cared about the art of baking.

FRIDAY NIGHT at the Pierce's. Louise had gone all out for my birthday that year, decorating the walls with cardboard cutouts of bobby soxers in various dance poses. A mural of an old-fashioned ice cream parlor hung on another wall. She rented a black and white checkered dance floor, filled the room with balloons, and weighed down the table with a smorgasbord of food and drink.

Like every gathering of law enforcement officers, the guest

list was mostly made up of police officers, detectives, and their significant others, along with the county coroner, the assistant district attorney, and a few law clerks. There was even a judge and a local representative snacking at the buffet table.

A few of the officers there were on call, but they still swung by for a little fun before having to pull away. Fortunately, the evening passed without anyone having to answer a call.

As the birthday boy, I was nominated to start the karaoke. Holding the mic, I started singing one of my favorites by Shep and the Limelites. I grabbed Louise by the hand and slowly twirled her around the dance floor.

She pulled away in the middle of my song to take the cake out of the fridge. By this time, everyone was singing.

Louise returned in time for my big finish. I dramatically opened my arms and sang my heart out to her.

The crowd clapped, hollered, and cheered.

My wife and I have quite a collection of Oldies but Goodies, the music of our teen years when we met. Whenever friends come over, they like to bombard us with questions in an attempt to test our knowledge of those old songs. This evening was no different. After taking turns on the karaoke machine, we decided to play music trivia.

"Did everyone do their research?" Detective Hanley asked.

"*Yes!*" the crowd boomed back.

"Excellent. Let the games begin! I'll go first." He took a slip of paper out of his pocket, looked it over, and asked, "Howard, who wrote Little Darlin?"

"The Diamonds, 1957," I answered without missing a beat.

"Twist and Shout," yelled the coroner.

"Tricky one, Bob. Written in 1961 by Phil Medley and Bert Berns, it was originally recorded by the Top Notes. But it was the Isley Brothers who made it a hit in 1962. Later, the Beatles also recorded it."

"Damn, Howard, you're such a show-off."

"Not a show-off, Bob, I just know my stuff."

He raised his glass in a salute.

"Anyone else?" I prompted.

"Ten Commandments of Love"

"1958, Harvey and the Moonglows."

"Sincerely"

"1954 by a young Marvin Gaye."

It was my wife's turn next.

"Okay Louise, who recorded Soldier Boy?" Celia asked from the buffet table, before taking a bite of cheese.

"The Shirelles in 1962, Ceci," she answered without hesitation.

"Mama Said."

"Shirelles. Same year."

"You two deserve one another," the district attorney called out, grinning.

But the testing wouldn't stop.

"The Great Pretender"

"Platters, 1955"

"Two Lovers"

"Mary Wells, 1962."

"All right, all right," interrupted Louise. Time for cake."

Louise went into the kitchen and came out carrying the cake, being careful to walk slowly lest the five brightly lit candles blow out.

"Hey, Howard, I didn't know you were only five years old today. Had I known, I would have bought you a toy," O'Malley said. Everyone howled.

"If Louise had put a candle for every year of my birth on the cake, she would have set it on fire," I said, amid the laughter. "Each candle represents a decade I've been alive."

"Very clever, Louise," disguising his true age," said O'Malley, winking conspiratorially, "But you left out four years."

"We just count decades, Sean. When he turns sixty, I'll add six candles to his cake." Louise said, smiling.

"Like I said, you're clever."

Louise took a little bow.

She pulled me by the hand and led me to stand in front of the cake.

"All right, everyone, gather around and let's sing."

A little embarrassed while everyone sang, I enjoyed every minute of it. I could not stop smiling.

After much eating, drinking, singing, and dancing, we closed the door on the last of our guests.

"Your birthday was a success," exclaimed Louise. "Did you enjoy it, Howie?"

"Are you kidding? It was terrific. Thank you for a great birthday. Come here," I said, scooping her toward me for a hug and kiss, before breaking into the lyrics of *A Teenager in Love*.

"Dion and the Belmonts, 1959," Louise said. We fell into a fit of laughter.

It was a little past two in the morning when we finally retired for the evening.

AT THAT VERY HOUR, a murderer sat on the bed, reading the Pocono Record by the light of a small bedside lamp. As she had done every night since the murder, she scoured the newspaper for any updates on the investigation. The last article, printed a few weeks after the murder, didn't have anything new to add. The police still had no clue as to the identity of the murderer.

At first, people in the area were naturally shocked and afraid that a cold-blooded killer was on the loose. Op Ed pieces filled the paper the first few days, coffee shops buzzing with the latest news. Everyone had an opinion. With no new updates, however, people started to forget about the crime, turning their attention to other matters.

Putting aside the paper, she yawned. She hadn't even updated her diary today. Exhausted, she turned off the light and hoped for sleep. She was still awake two hours later, tossing and turning. Frustrated, she threw off the covers and got out of bed. Although the paper hadn't reported anything new, she had enough thoughts to fill a page or two in her diary.

As daylight invaded, shadows stretched across the room, eventually reaching the woman who had been sitting at her desk since before dawn.

Record keeping over, she pulled out a pair of latex gloves from the box in the desk drawer. Thinking of what she was going to write, she slowly put on the gloves, making sure all fingers were stretched comfortably. Satisfied, she took an index card from a stack on top of the desk. Reaching for her special red pen, she began to fill the card with familiar symbols. When she was finished, she slid the index card into an envelope and sealed it with one of those little water bottles with the sponge on the lid. Once stamped and addressed, the envelope was ready to be mailed.

She placed the pen back in its holder and set the envelope on the desk. Languidly stretching, she pulled off the gloves and trudged back to bed.

Maybe I'll lay down for an hour or so before getting ready to go to the bakery and start the machines, she thought sleepily, drifting off soon as her head hit the pillow.

23

WELROD PISTOL

Months into our investigation, Detective Leung came into my office holding some papers.

"Sarge, I've been doing some research on the type of gun used in the Romero case."

"Yes?"

"Did you know bolt-action guns are usually rifles?"

I knew Leung well enough to know once he started quizzing me about firearms, a lecture wouldn't be far behind.

"No Jun. I did not," I answered, amused.

"It's true, Sarge. There are some bolt-action pistols out there too, but it's rare to find one that fires quietly," he declared with a glint in his eye.

"Really?" I leaned back into my chair, intrigued.

"Yes, really," he paused, a hint of a smile tugging at the corners of his lips.

"I'm listening."

"I might have found a match for the weapon used in the Romero homicide."

He could barely contain his enthusiasm.

"Have a seat and tell me all about it."

"Read the first page," he said. He pushed the papers in front of me, taking a seat.

As I read, a familiar feeling began to tickle my stomach. He was onto something, and I could see why he was excited. He'd given me a description of a gun called the Welrod pistol, developed by the British during World War II. Its advanced noise suppression technology meant it remained quiet when fired, producing a sound somewhere between twenty-five to thirty-five decibels. More importantly, it was also designed as a nine-millimeter model.

I glanced up to find Detective Leung had inched himself closer to my desk. "Possible, right?" he asked, eagerness written all over his face.

"Possible, yes, but let's not get ahead of ourselves." His face fell.

"But this is certainly worth looking into," I added, seeing his disappointment. "Good job, Jun."

He sat taller.

I placed the descriptive sheet neatly on top of the pile.

"Follow me."

I stepped into the squad room, Detective Leung behind me.

"Listen up guys," I called.

"We have a possible lead on the weapon in the Romero case. It's an antique gun called the Welrod pistol. Might be why we haven't had any luck locating a viable firearm thus far. It's probably a collector's item, so it might not appear on any database unless it was used in a previous crime. Jun here will lead the search."

I returned to my desk, leaving a happy Junjie Leung in charge.

Further reading indicated the last reported usage for this weapon took place during Desert Storm, which made it a real challenge to find.

Detective Leung certainly had his work cut out for him.

Meanwhile, Detective O'Malley had been working diligently to find a boot that matched the footprint left at the crime scene.

In anticipation for authorization to obtain copies of sales receipts, O'Malley first contacted the magistrate's office. Warrant in his pocket, he began his quest for a pair of boots he believed would fit the distinctive sole pattern of the print left at the crime scene.

He picked up the warrants and hit the pavement running, visiting every store on his list.

His last stop of the day was at a shop specializing in hunting equipment and clothing. O'Malley examined the soles of every pair of the many boots displayed on the racks along the wall, until he found what he was looking for.

"This Polar Vortex boot is not only waterproof and well insulated, but the sixteen rubber studs on the sole are great for traction," the saleswoman had claimed. He could see why a person intent on braving the elements might want to choose this type of footwear.

O'Malley carefully compared his purchase with the forensic picture of the footprint. The sole pattern perfectly matched.

He stretched and rubbed his hands together, contemplating the mound of paperwork he acquired from the shop owner, dating back several years.

Now it was time for the nitty-gritty—going through the pile, finding buyers to question, and hopefully coming up with a suspect. This was going to be a long process. The first step was to determine if the purchases were made by out-of-towners or locals. How many of these people were hunters, skiers, hikers, or outdoor workers? And had they bought the boots for personal use or as gifts?

O'Malley interviewed anyone who lived nearby in person, and by telephone if they did not.

Three and a half weeks later, he narrowed his search to two buyers he wanted to scrutinize closer.

· · ·

WE BROUGHT in two different people named Anna for questioning, although neither of their last names was Mont.

I immediately recognized the first-person O'Malley escorted into the interrogation room.

"Please sit, Miss Wagner," he said, pointing to the chair opposite him.

She hesitated, looking around the room and nervously staring at the bar bolted to the table to handcuff prisoners to. She made a show of plopping her purse on top of the table with a loud thud, taking her time as she undid the buttons of her jacket. Finally, she slouched down in the chair and crossed her arms.

O'Malley waited patiently. He clicked on the tape recorder as soon as she was settled.

"What am I doing here?" she asked, looking up at the camera mounted high on the wall. "I have a business to run."

"We're sorry for the inconvenience, ma'am."

"Bet you are." O'Malley ignored her comment.

"Before we begin, would you like water or a cup of coffee?"

She let out an exasperated breath. "No. Just get this over with. I have to get back to the bakery, like I said."

"All right. I'll get right to it then. Miss Wagner, we are investigating the murder of Mr. Felix Romero. We brought you in to clear up a few things."

"Who? You mean that guy who was murdered in his own home? What's that got to do with me?"

"That's what we're here to determine."

She turned her head and stared directly at the two-way mirror, sensing someone was watching from the other side. Her stare grew colder, and more scathing as she pretended to ignore her interrogator.

"Will you please look at me, Miss Wagner?" instructed O'Malley.

Reluctantly, she tore her eyes away from the mirror.

Why the animosity?

"I understand on the morning of Saturday, February fifteenth, you were involved in an argument at your place of business with one of your customers," O'Malley stated.

"Really? I don't recall."

"Witnesses said the argument ended when Mr. Romero threw a bagel at you and stormed out of your store."

"Oh, him," she replied, uncrossing her arms, and flicking her hand dismissively. "Yes, I remember. A very nasty thing to do."

"Mr. Romero was found dead next morning," said O'Malley, his expression impartial. She straightened up from her slouch, suddenly concerned.

"Hold on. You think just because a customer throws a fit in my store that it's motive enough for me to kill him? Are you kidding me?"

"I am not kidding. We checked, and on the very next morning somebody assassinated Mr. Romero, you were not at the bakery at your usual time of eight AM."

She bit at her bottom lip, weighing her answer. "Was that the weekend when that terrible blizzard hit the Poconos?"

"Yes. I believe it was."

"I opened an hour early that Saturday, at seven. I wanted to make sure the plow drivers could get breakfast somewhere before beginning their shift," she said, smiling. "I'm thoughtful that way."

"That's commendable," my guy answered, still straight-faced. She sat a little more comfortably.

"Yes, I remember. The day after that man almost took my eye out, I felt a little sick—over-tired is more like it, so I decided to sleep later than usual. I called my assistant and had her open the shop for me. She usually comes in at six anyway to start the baking."

"Will she verify that?"

"Ask her." Miss Wagner's attitude had returned.

"What is your assistant's name?"

"Lill."

"Lill?"

"That's what I said."

"Got a last name for Lill?"

"Gil."

Gil? I've heard that name before.

"So her name is Lill Gil?" asked O'Malley stifling the urge to laugh.

"Have you ever heard of nicknames? she asked, exasperated. "I call her Lill. Her first name is Lillian, obviously."

"You wouldn't happen to have her home number, would you?" he asked, unfazed by her sarcasm.

She took a moment before replying. "Sure, Detective. Let me look it up in my address book."

"I'd appreciate that."

She reached into her purse and pulled out a red address book.

The red address book got me thinking. The crime scene note was written in red ink as well as notes sent to me. Her pastries all have red piping, even the bakery is associated with the color. Is the damn color a clue, or is it just a coincidence?

Miss Wagner paged through her book, found the number, and pushed the book across the table. "Here it is."

Detective O'Malley jotted down the information.

"Thank you," he said, pushing it towards her.

Wagner seized the address book and shoved it back inside her purse.

This woman does not like to be questioned.

O'Malley referred to his pad. "You bought a pair of winter boots, size eleven wide on February second. For yourself?" he asked.

"What? Yes, of course for myself. Why? Is there a law against buying boots for yourself?"

"No Ma'am, no law against that. What size shoes do you wear?"

"Size ten."

O'Malley waited for her to connect the dots.

She raised an eyebrow and cocked her head to the side, challenging him to continue.

When he remained silent, she realized what he was waiting for. "Oh, I see. You want to know why I bought boots in a bigger size."

"That would be helpful."

She rolled her eyes. "I like men's boots because they're wider and more comfortable. I wear them with two pairs of thick socks."

"I see." Are you a runner, Miss Wagner?"

"Yes. I like to keep in shape," she responded with obvious pride.

"How often do you run?"

"As often as I can."

"Did you go for a run on Sunday, February sixteenth?"

"How am I supposed to remember? That was months ago."

"The same morning you slept later than usual," he fired back expressionless.

She slid her chair back in a huff. "Are you trying to trick me? Why would I go running if I felt too tired to go to work? How much longer is this going to take anyway? I have to get back to the bakery."

"Not much longer." He paused and wrote something in his pad, making her fidget in her seat.

"You opened your business a little over ten years ago. Did you move here, or are you a local?"

She inhaled deeply before answering. "I moved here from New York City where I'd lived all my life."

"Any particular reason you decided to move?"

"No. Ads said come to the Poconos and I came," she said, with all the sarcasm she could muster.

"Yes, everyone wants to come to the Poconos," O'Malley said, without skipping a beat.

"What high school did you attend in the city?"

"How is knowing what damn high school I attended relevant?"

"Please answer the question."

She gave him a look dripping with animosity. "Fine. Mabel Dean Bacon to study cosmetology, but I couldn't wait to get the hell out of there."

"Did you study stenography?"

"No, just cosmetology, like I said. You need to brush up on your listening skills."

"Where did you learn how to bake?" he asked, ignoring her comment.

"Self-taught. Took lots of books out of the library on cake baking and decorating. I practiced, and I learned."

"That's admirable."

"Oh gee, thanks. Can I go now?" she scowled.

Just a couple more questions. "Any reason your desserts are decorated with the color red?"

"That's an obvious one, Detective. I love the color. Goes with everything."

"You gave the store an unusual name, also because of your love for the color red, is that correct?"

"Yes. Is there a law against that too?"

"None that I can think of."

A vein began to pulse in the side of her forehead. She was getting madder by the minute. O'Malley kept pushing.

"Do you own a gun, Miss Wagner?"

"I do not."

"Are you sure?"

"I think I should know if I owned a gun. I already told you, no."

"I'll ask you one more time. Do you own a gun, Miss

Wagner? And before you answer, you should know, lying to me will not sit well for you."

She gritted her teeth, face turning a beet red. "*I. Said. No.*"

"We have enough probable cause to search your home and business."

"You're arresting me?" she blurted, taken aback.

"Not at the present time. Police will escort you to your home and business where a search will be conducted. They will provide you with a copy of the search warrant. Good day, Ma'am."

Detective O'Malley switched off the tape recorder and strode over to open the door. A moment of fear flashed across Miss Wagner's face when he called in the officers who were waiting to escort her out of the precinct.

A few minutes later, the next Anna arrived. She stood five feet, three-inches tall at most, and wore a size six shoe. Not only was she short, but she was also significantly overweight, and asthmatic. I doubted she could have taken down Mr. Romero. We ran a background check on her just in case. As expected, it came up empty. This Anna had grown up in Jersey City, New Jersey, and had lived in East Stroudsburg for the last fifteen years. More importantly, she had a solid alibi for the night of the murder. She had been miles away in Phoenixville, Pennsylvania, attending a family wedding.

"I have a photo in my purse if you'd like to see it," she said, pulling out a date-stamped photograph before I could answer. There she was, standing with the happy couple on the night of the Romero homicide.

Couldn't hit a homerun every time.

24

THE BLOODHOUND

The search of Anna Wagner's properties did not yield any incriminating evidence to implicate her in the murder of Mr. Felix Romero. Her assistant confirmed she had opened the shop herself on the date in question, while Wagner slept in.

In the meantime, I verified Anna Wagner as the sole proprietor of the Rufescent Confectionary. She had started her business back in 1970 under the name, Wagner's Odds and Ends, a novelty store selling greeting cards, candy, all sorts of gag toys, and some cakes and cookies she purchased from the local supermarket. When the novelty store consistently failed to make a profit, she decided to turn her business into the only bakery in town.

As the local population grew, the competition wasn't far behind. One by one, her abused and underpaid bakers, quit, and went elsewhere. And yet, according to tax records, the Rufescent had become very successful over the past few years.

Back to the drawing board.

That afternoon, during one of our brainstorming sessions, Detective O'Malley came up with another avenue to explore.

"My investigation has resulted in a person of interest," he announced.

Pausing for dramatic effect, O'Malley pulled a piece of paper from his file folder. "I have here a receipt dated January second for a pair of size eleven Polar Vortex boots sold to Mr. Lowell Adler of 2224 Birdview Lane."

Polar Vortex boots? Those definitely were not the boots I saw in Adler's closet.

"Good job, Sean," I commented. "Why don't you pay Mr. Adler a visit?"

"Will do."

"Anyone else have anything new?"

"I do," said Byrne.

"What's that, Ceci?"

"I kept digging into the Romero's finances, and discovered, for a period of twenty-one months in the seventies, Mr. Romero was paying rent for a furnished apartment on the upper west side of Manhattan. Not his legal residence."

She paused and cleared her throat. "Either Mr. Romero had a secret love nest, or...No, that's it. It was a love nest."

Everyone laughed.

"Tell me you found someone who lived there at the time," I hopefully asked.

"I sure did, Sarge. I tracked down the super." Celia referred to her notebook. "A Mr. Lawrence, who serviced the building in the seventies and eighties. He's retired now, but he still lives in the building. Mr. Lawrence and I had a nice chat on the phone. Boy, that man likes to talk. I had a hell of a time getting him to stay on topic—guess he doesn't get many phone calls. Nice old man though."

"How sweet," O'Malley teased.

"He said he remembered Romero because he was never late on a rent payment, and he always paid with crisp, new bills. That's why I couldn't find it at first—he was paying cash, but you know me. I kept digging until I discovered monthly cash withdrawals from an individual checking account at a different bank from the one where the Romeros had their joint account. Deposits were automatically made through his company's payroll department. And get this," she said, flipping a page on her notepad. "The account was in the name of Fernando Romero, his son, who was a minor at the time."

"Great work, Detective. Anything else?"

Yes, she said, "The cash withdrawals were made on the same day each month while he was renting the apartment."

"Did the super ever see Mr. Romero with anyone?"

Celia tossed her long hair out of her eyes. "As a matter of fact, he did. He said even though Mr. Romero was the one who rented and paid for the apartment, a very pretty redhead lived there. Romero came by frequently, but as far as the super could tell, he never stayed overnight. He assumed the redhead was Romero's girlfriend. He described her as having red hair, nice eyes, of average height, looked to be in her twenties. Oh, and he said she looked strong."

"Strong? How so?"

"He said she was fit, not an ounce of fat on her," she shrugged. "I don't know. That's what he said."

"Were you able to get a name?"

"Fraid not. She wasn't very friendly, according to Mr. Lawrence. He told me he said hi to her once and she completely ignored him, so he never spoke to her again."

"All right. Keep investigating that lead."

"You bet."

I waited for the room to settle down again before briefly filling them in on Romero's revelation.

"Fernando Romero recounted his mother's confession to him of an affair her husband had, which coincides with Celia's time frame. Could be an old flame has popped up and taken revenge for some strife committed years ago. Let's see if we can find her."

I searched their faces. Some were nodding, looking

thoughtful, while others wore grins, as they sensed they might finally discover a motive.

"Anyone else have something?"

No one spoke.

"Okay then, back to work. I'm stepping out for a while. I need a minute to clear my head. Iggy, take over, will you?"

"Aye, Sir," he responded with a salute.

"Wise guy."

As I turned onto Ann Street I spotted both Mr. Adler and Miss Wagner out in front of the Ribbon Factory, stretching after a run, I assumed. They had a brief conversation, before hugging and parting ways. They got into their respective vehicles and drove away in different directions.

That was interesting.

I hurried back to my car and drove straight to the station, where I dialed Detective Jones.

"Howard. Nice to hear from you again. How can I help you?"

"I just have a quick question for you, if you don't mind."

"No, of course not. What is it?"

"In your Mont investigation, did the victim's niece have red hair?"

"Yes. Red hair and hazel eyes."

"You wouldn't happen to have a picture, would you?"

"Didn't I include one in the folder I gave you?"

"Not that I saw."

"Oh, sorry about that. I'll email a copy to you soon as I hang up."

"Thanks, Fred."

"You're welcome. Sounds like you might be onto something."

"I hope so. Talk to you soon."

The email pinged in my inbox a minute later. When I opened it, Anna Mont's face filled my desktop. As I studied the image, I noticed her eyes did not smile along with her mouth. She struck me as an incredibly sad girl.

A person's face can change a lot over the years, but the eyes stay the same. Not only was Mont's bone structure significantly different than Anna Wagner's, but her eyes were bigger and shaped differently.

I opened the web browser and began to research old high school yearbooks for Charles Evans Hughes High School from 1965 through 1968. I wanted to check if Mr. Adler had attended the same school during the time Miss Mont was there. He had not, and neither had Miss Wagner. As a matter of fact, I found the bakery owner in one of Mabel Dean Bacon High School yearbooks from the sixties. She had indeed taken a course in cosmetology.

If any of these people had known each other before moving here, I could not find a connection.

I stuck my head out my office door. "Ramirez, would you please put a tail on both Anna Wagner and Lowell Adler?"

For the next few weeks they were seen running and chatting, never visiting each other at home, or behaving suspiciously in any way. Their routine was pretty much set — they would meet at the Y on Main Street, run together, and then part ways. Adler went to the bakery once a week, each time walking out with a bakery box after only a few minutes. Undoubtedly, Wagner didn't make him wait.

The boots turned out to be a birthday gift for Lowell Adler's childhood friend, who was an avid hunter. Mr. Adler still had a thank-you email describing the gift, received a couple of days after his friend got the FedEx package containing the boots.

I continued to study the file Detective Jones had given me every chance I got, desperate to find a clue that could help me identify Mr. Romero's killer.

Ramirez's Aunt Maddy continued to decipher all of the mail periodically sent to my attention. She had gotten adept at capturing the gist of those notes, all of which taunted my investigation and primarily me, the bloodhound, as the killer referred to me.

Bloodhound. I kind of liked the moniker, if I'm being honest.

Winter gave way to spring and spring gave way to summer, but we were still no closer to solving this case. As summer drew to a close, I began to worry I'd have to postpone my retirement only six months away.

We took on another homicide investigation during that frustrating time, and the full caseload limited the amount of time we could devote to the Romero homicide.

By that November, the case was getting colder and colder.

25

JUN'S PHONE CALL

The birds' morning song pushed all thoughts of the Romero case out of my mind. I'd been sitting in my den for the past hour, ever since devouring Louise's special weekend breakfast of blueberry waffles, Canadian bacon, fresh-squeezed orange juice, and freshly ground, whole bean coffee. Yes, I really did buy a coffee grinder soon after visiting Mr. Adler. It makes a huge difference in the taste, but it also makes it difficult for me to stop at only two cups. Good thing Louise keeps a watchful eye on me.

I'd been mulling over the particulars of what we knew so far regarding the investigation. Needing a breather, I swiveled my chair to get a better look out the window, hoping to spot the finches that occasionally visited my property. You'd think I'd be used to all this natural beauty after so many years in the Poconos, but the panorama before me took my breath away. The snow-covered trees glistened like diamonds in bright sunlight after the dangerous ice storm of the night before. The landscape looked clean and peaceful.

Out of the corner of my eye, I saw a pair of our hardy Pocono finches fly straight for the bird feeder. They perched on either side pecking at the seeds, dropping more than they consumed. Louise christened these two beauties Sonny and Cher the first year they came to visit. We look forward to seeing them every year.

As I watched the birds, I noticed a small family of deer stroll by, leaving evidence of their trek on the snow. As I stared at nature's mural, I wondered how people could complain about this weather. Yes, it can be harsh at times, but nothing can compare with the beauty of the changing seasons in this region. I wouldn't move to a warmer climate if you paid me. Of course, I grew up here, so I guess I'm acclimated to the changing weather conditions.

Feeling somewhat refreshed, I turned away from the window and picked up the damp newspaper I'd brought in earlier. The pages were filled with familiar photographs and stories, the kind they publish after every storm — accidents, downed trees, electrical wires on the roads, and a listing of neighborhoods with power outages.

I made it halfway through the paper when my wife strutted in and bamboozled me.

"Howie, I was thinking," she began, never directly accusing me of procrastinating. "We still haven't opened that box delivered weeks ago."

"Yeah. We need to do that," I said, flipping to the next page of the paper.

"Don't you think we should make sure it wasn't damaged in transit?" she persisted. "Just in case there's a problem, and we have to return it."

"Uh huh. Good thinking," I mumbled, without putting down the paper. I enjoy toying with her.

Louise waited for a second, five seconds, ten seconds. "Is the box cutter in a worktable drawer?" she finally asked.

That's my girl!

I folded the newspaper, placed it on the desk, and got out of my chair. I turned toward my wife, who had been watching me intently.

"Follow me, please. I'll show you where I keep the box cutter."

"Okay," she sweetly responded, knowing full well I would be spending the afternoon building her bookcase. That woman knew me so well.

I grabbed a sweater from the closet and offered it to my clever wife.

"Here, better put this on. It's chilly in there."

She grabbed the sweater and smiled. "Thank you, Sweetie."

When she was ready, I opened the door, flicked on the overhead light, and walked over to the worktable, Louise close behind.

"There's the box cutter," I announced, pointing to the corkboard.

"Thanks," she said uncertainly. She leaned over the table to grab the blade, but I caught her arm before she could do so.

"Now you know I can't take the chance you might cut yourself slitting that box open. Let me do it."

"Are you sure?" she asked, eyes twinkling.

"I'm sure."

"Oh, and Howie?" she said coyly. "Once you get the box open, you might as well put the thing together."

"Yes, dear. My thoughts exactly."

Louise moved closer and wrapped her arms around me, kissing my waiting lips.

"Best husband ever," she whispered. I smiled broadly.

"I love you too."

She sauntered into the house, a happy woman. Only took her three weeks to give me a nudge. That woman has the patience of Job.

First thing I did was turn on the electric heater on the wall, then I opened the garage door and moved my car into the driveway so I would have enough space to work. Back inside, I turned on the radio and pressed the preset button for the oldies station.

The song, *Shop Around,* by the Miracles, streamed out of the speakers. *Ah, a good one,* I thought, singing along.

I grabbed the box cutter off the corkboard and checked the blade. It was dull.

I dug through one of the bins and found a box of new blades. Humming along to the tune on the radio, I unwrapped a blade and replaced the old one, dancing my way over to the carton.

Three long swipes of the cutter, and the cardboard fell away from the contents inside.

I carefully lifted the panels and shelves and stacked them to one side, placing the small plastic bag of hardware on top of the pile. I picked up Styrofoam and cardboard, stuffed them into a large garbage bag and reached for the broom and dustpan.

Floor cleaned, I noticed the large booklet with big, bold letters labeled, INSTRUCTIONS. I groaned. Not a simple, one-pager one might expect when putting together a small, uncomplicated bookcase.

Oh, man. I hope I can finish this by game time.

At my worktable, instruction manual and baggy in hand, I switched on the lamp and turned to the first page. There was a diagram describing all the hardware needed for the project, tagged with an assigned number for each part. All the pieces corresponded with the wood panel of the same number.

Makes sense so far.

I then slit open the plastic bag assuring all the necessary parts were included and matched the diagram on the Description-of-Contents page.

Everything matches. Good.

Thumbing through the manual to get an idea of what was in store for me, I was pleasantly surprised.

Most of these pages are instructions in other languages, of course.

The job looked easier than I first imagined. Satisfied, I grabbed the bag and instructions, and strode over to the pile on the floor. Sitting cross-legged, I reached for the wood panels and arranged them by letter. I took out the many components from the bag and lined them up by size. Once I had everything organized, I began putting the case together, all the while singing along to the radio.

Easy Peasey, I thought, as I finished screwing in the last panel.

Now for the shelves.

I picked up a washer, ready to insert a screw into the shelf, when a thought crossed my mind. Aren't guns made up of different parts? An old weapon like the Welrod pistol probably has more pieces than modern guns.

Once the thought had entered my mind, I couldn't stop thinking about it.

I began to sing along with the Tokens' *The Lion Sleeps Tonight*, a favorite of mine, to keep my mind off the gun. I'd never finish the bookcase if I let myself get distracted. I tightened a bolt on the first shelf.

Just as I bellowed the last line of the song, Louise walked in. *Uh oh.*

"Howie, Detective Leung is on the phone." I sighed, relieved. For a split second, I thought she was going to complain about my loud singing.

"Be right there. Thanks, Hon."

Louise gave the bookcase the once over. "Looking good, Sweetie. Thank you," she said, blowing me a kiss before leaving.

"My pleasure."

"Don't keep the detective waiting."

"I won't."

I gave the bolt a last hard twist and headed in to my den.

"Hi, Jun. What's up?" I asked, leaning back in my chair, and putting my feet up on my desk.

"Howard," he excitedly said. "You'll never guess what I've just discovered."

"What?" I inquired, sensing his excitement.

"I just came from a gun show where I got into a very interesting conversation with a gun dealer who's as passionate a collector as I am."

Gun dealer? Don't get your hopes up, Howard.

"Really?" I asked, as casually as I could.

"Yeah. I asked him if he ever heard of the Welrod pistol. He said he knew the weapon well and had wanted to own one for a long time. Said he came close a few years back." Jun paused for effect. I could imagine the wide grin splashed across his face.

"I'm listening."

I knew I was making the right choice when I assigned the search for the Welrod to Detective Leung, who's been a member of the National Rifle Association for as long as I've known him. He's an avid gun collector who spends most of his free time scouring gun shows. If anyone were going to find the elusive gun, it would be him.

"He told me about the time he met up with a woman at a gun show. He called it a date, at least, but I have my doubts," he snorted. "Anyway, he said he didn't know what to talk about. He said he's shy."

Detective Leung, on the other hand, found it easy to make new friends, especially if they shared his passion for firearms.

"Naturally, he began to show off his extensive weapons knowledge," Jun laughed heartily. "Almost as good as mine, but not quite," he boasted.

I laughed along with him. My weapons expert is a walking encyclopedia when it comes to firearms.

Leung cleared his throat. "Vic said his date seemed interested and encouraging, so he confessed his dream of owning a Welrod."

He paused. "Are you ready for the best part, Howard?"

"Can't wait, Jun." I found his excitement infectious.

"She told him she owned a Welrod. "Ain't that a kicker, Sarge?"

I took my feet off the desk and leaned forward in my chair. "I'll say."

I put him on speaker, and got up to pace, anxious for him to tie it all together already. I learned a long time ago not to rush Detective Leung lest he forget details, so I paced.

"He said he couldn't believe it. As you read from the web pages I gave you, it's a pretty heavy piece of equipment. You need two hands to handle it. This gun's sole purpose is to get up close and personal to your victim and kill him quietly. They don't call it an assassin's weapon for nothing, Sarge. Not what you'd call a ladies' gun."

I held my breath knowing Jun wouldn't have called me if he didn't have something tangible.

"Vic said something along those lines to the woman, and the next thing he knew, she grabbed him by the arms and said, and I'm quoting here, 'You calling me a liar?' I laughed so hard when he told me that part. Imagine such a big guy getting man handled, or should I say, woman handled? Hilarious!"

I was getting more impatient by the minute.

"Well, did she or didn't she own a Welrod?" I asked a bit harshly.

"I'm getting to that, Sarge," he said, sounding hurt.

"Sorry, Jun. Didn't mean to sound annoyed."

"That's all right, the best part is coming up," he said with renewed enthusiasm.

Yes, there's a best part. I resumed pacing.

"Vic challenged her and said, 'Anyone can say they own a Welrod, but seeing is believing.' He said her face contorted until all he could see were slits where her eyes should be. He tore himself from her grasp and was about to walk away when she dared him to follow her to her house so she could prove she owned the gun. He agreed, but he said he got nervous on the way there. Something about her was off."

"Off, how?" I asked, with added interest.

"That look of hers, gave him the willies, and he's a brawny tough guy, or so he claims. He almost turned the car around and bailed on the whole thing. Lucky for us, the hope of seeing a Welrod up close was too strong a temptation for him."

I briefly closed my eyes and pinched the bridge of my nose.

"Howard…she wasn't lying," said Leung, lowering his voice almost to a whisper.

Finally, the point to this story. I wiped the sweat off my brow with the back of my hand, my heart racing.

"Did she mention where she got the gun?" I blurted.

"She said she inherited the gun from an uncle who died in the war."

"And was he successful acquiring the pistol after all that?"

"Nah. She flatly refused to sell it to him."

My shoulders sagged, and I stopped pacing, feeling the tension building throughout my body.

Detective Leung continued to drag out whatever else he wanted me to know.

"Vic said he offered her all the money he had in the bank, but she wouldn't budge. Said no amount of money could get her to part with such a treasure. She threw him out when he kept pushing," Leung chuckled.

"And you checked PICS to see if the state police have a record of a sale in the database, right?" I asked as I resumed pacing.

"You know it, but no luck there."

"Did your friend happen to remember the address?" I asked hopefully.

"Saved the best for last, Sarge."

I stopped pacing.

"You're not going to believe it when I tell you where she lives."

"Where, Jun?"

I wrote down the name and address, shaking my head. I had been right—the assailant walked to the Romero house. The tension left my body as quickly as it had risen.

"You did good, Jun. Real good."

"Thanks. Talk to you later."

Feeling lighter than I had in many months, I made a note to contact the National Archives for Veterans' Records. Perhaps we would find a soldier who served in World War II and is related to our now, number-one suspect.

I was just about to lay the pencil down, when it occurred to me further research of the pension payment records might also lead us to a next of kin.

Look into pension payment records, I jotted on my notepad. It was an extremely long shot, but we were in the business of following long shots.

I realized this search could take weeks to sift through. I would need to talk to the team about it first thing Monday morning, grateful we were definitely moving in the right direction.

I glanced at my watch. Plenty of time before the game to finish that bookcase.

26
—————

THE SEARCH

Since we still didn't have proof the Welrod was the
murder weapon, I held off visiting our suspect until we
could come up with a connection to Felix Romero.

My patience paid off. A couple of weeks later, we
unearthed the lead that cracked the case wide open.

A search of The National Archives yielded information on
an officer who served with the OSS, the intelligence agency
operating in Europe during the Second World War. His name
was Gregory Mont, killed in action in 1944 during the Battle of
Monte Casino in Italy.

From the research we'd done on the Welrod, I knew it was
a popular assassin's weapon in the covert operations in Europe
during that time.

I felt safe to assume Mont acquired the Welrod during his
time with the OSS.

"Keep digging, fellas. We're not there yet," I urged, seeing
the finish line.

Along with military records, we also obtained copies of his
birth, death, and marriage certificates.

Gregory Mont had married Jessica Gil in 1943, three days
before shipping off to war.

As I went through Officer Mont's records, I focused first on his wife's maiden name. The name Gil kept popping up during the course of the investigation.

I slapped my forehead. *Damn!*

"O'Malley," I shouted from my desk. "Would you please come here?"

"Yes, boss?" he asked, stepping into my office. He was looking distinctly disheveled with his untucked shirt stretched to its limit around his generous belly, a pencil behind his left ear, and reading glasses precariously balancing at the tip of his nose.

"O'Malley, isn't there an employee named Gil working at the Rufescent bakery?"

He rubbed his chin. "Can't say off the top of my head but let me check my notes. Be right back."

He returned a few minutes later with his notebook in hand. Pushing his glasses further up his nose, he rifled through the pages until he found what he was looking for.

"Here it is. Yes, police interviewed a Miss Lillian Gil at the bakery."

"Anything relevant?"

"Only that she was the one who opened the shop on the morning of Romero's homicide, confirming her boss called to say she wasn't feeling well."

"By the way, Miss Gil is also a neighbor of the Romeros," O'Malley said, sifting through his notes. "Police interviewed her on that first day of the investigation."

"Oh shit. How did we miss that?"

"No reason to peg her as a suspect at the time, Sarge," he said, scanning his notes. "Miss Gil was visiting with Mrs. Romero when Mr. Romero came home. Mrs. Romero tried to introduce her, but the mister was drunk. Said he gave her a dirty look. She left and never went back."

So Miss Gil had been in the Romero house previous to the

homicide. On how many occasions? I wondered. Enough times to study the layout?

O'Malley glanced at me over the rim of his glasses. "Remember, the owner of the bakery was the focus on the day we searched her house and business."

"Yes. Not blaming you. I didn't connect the dots either."

He closed his pad and waited for any further questions I might have.

"Thanks, Sean."

"Sure thing," he said heading back to his desk.

I reached for the file from Detective Jones, shaking my head when I discovered the name Gil had been there all along, almost taunting me. I whistled softly, not surprised we'd missed this. Sometimes we get so bogged down in paperwork we miss what should have been obvious.

Our number one suspect's name is Lillian Gil. The names Mont and Gil are both unusual names.

Romero's neighbor, a baker, possibly connected to a victim in an unsolved case with the name Gil, is too much of a coincidence. This had to be an important piece of the puzzle getting us closer to solving this crime.

I slammed the file down and reached for the telephone. We had our suspect. I knew it.

"Pick up, pick up," I mumbled.

Once I explained I had probable cause for a search, the Magisterial District judge agreed to issue a warrant. "Thank you," I hastily uttered before hanging up. I typed up the affidavit and gathered the necessary paperwork for the warrant, grabbing my coat, and looking for Detective Leung. "Follow me," I requested when I found him.

We stopped at the judge's office to secure the warrant before heading to Birdview Lane.

"This is how we're going to play it," I explained on the way to the suspect's residence. "The warrant only gives us the right to look for the weapon, but we might uncover other evidence while we search. If you see something useful, jot it down and we'll go over it later."

"Boss. This isn't my first rodeo, you know?" Leung reminded me.

"Sorry, I know. It's just, we're so close, I don't want to miss anything."

"Relax, Sarge. We got this," he assured me.

We pounded on the suspect's door a few times before a woman's voice called out for us to wait a moment.

Good. She's home.

At times like these you don't know what to expect. We stood on either side of the door, mentally prepared for any dangerous situation that might arise. We'd called for backup while en route. The patrol car arrived just as we got there.

After a minute, the occupant of the house answered the door. There she stood—five feet ten, slender, freckled-faced, with hazel eyes, fringed by thin crows-feet lines, and dark brown hair in need of a dye job. I could spot red strands along her hairline. She looked to be in her middle fifties, an older version of her high school picture.

"May I help you?" she inquired, none too friendly.

"Miss Lillian Gil?"

"Yes?"

I cocked my head toward my partner. "This is Detective Leung. I'm Detective Pierce."

No reaction. *She's not surprised.*

"We have a search warrant for a weapon called the Welrod pistol," I said, reaching into my coat pocket for the document.

Miss Gil stared from the police standing behind us back to me. Without another word, she tugged the door open wide, stepping aside to let us in. She held out her hand for the warrant but didn't bother to read it. Instead she folded it twice and stuffed it in her pants pocket.

"If you would please show us the weapon we wouldn't need

to search your home," I said, knowing already I was wasting my breath.

"What weapon?" she asked in mocked innocence.

"All right," I shrugged, turning toward the officers. "Begin the search, fellas."

"Tell your men not to mess up my house," she snapped.

"Please sit, Ma'am, while my men do their job."

Her cold, emotionless eyes burrowed into mine, before she casually walked into the living room. She picked up a magazine and pencil off the side table and began filling in what I assumed to be a crossword puzzle.

She's a cool one.

Looking around the living room from where I stood, I noticed there was not a single picture or knickknack in that austere room.

I walked away and stopped by a small hallway closet filled with outer garments. I leafed through them but didn't find a down coat, just a couple of plain wool coats and various sweaters and scarfs. On the floor were two pairs of running shoes and a well-worn pair of leather boots. Unfortunately, upon closer inspection, they were not the boots O'Malley had described. Nevertheless, I checked the inside label—size ten and a half. I put down the boot, closed the door, and headed upstairs.

I entered a bedroom on the second floor. Although it was the middle of the afternoon, the room was dark. I reached for the light switch and was shocked to find the walls were painted a deep ominous red, bordered by an even darker shade of red. *Wow, creepy.*

Standing by the doorway, I surveyed the dour room. The dark, cherry-wood furniture almost blended into the walls. The floor was covered in a faded black and yellow linoleum with a rust-colored area rug by the bed.

In all my years on the force, I had never seen a bedroom so steeped in gloom. It felt like something out of an old horror movie. The only other colors in that room were on the bed, where she had laid a faded yellow bedspread over the sheets and mattress. An old, ragged doll wearing a wrinkled and stained red dress was propped up against the three pillows in various pastel colors, neatly stacked along the headboard.

She runs hot and cold, I thought. *Polarized*.

An alarm clock, lamp, and CD player were organized on the nightstand. Opposite the window, an oval mirror with a dark red frame hung towards the edge of the wall. *Strange place for a mirror*.

Again, like the living room, there were no photos or mementos anywhere.

The top of the dresser was bare. No makeup or perfume of any kind, not even a comb or hairbrush. I walked toward the dresser and passed my hand over the surface. Not a speck of dust. I opened drawers and found a comb, hairbrush, and hair clips. The others were neatly packed with night clothes and underwear. Being very careful not to disturb the garments, I felt around underneath, in case she had the gun hidden in her dresser. She did not.

An old secretary desk with a roll top caught my attention. I wandered over and picked up a hardcover notebook off the desk. My heart skipped a beat when I opened the book. It looked to be a diary of some kind. It was filled with shorthand entries, some pages dated. I placed it back on the desk.

A stack of index cards filled one of the open cubbies. In another, envelopes. A small water bottle with a sponge top was positioned in a third cubby. I picked up a pen from the holder on the desk and saw it had a red tip.

This is where she writes the notes she taunts me with.

Although the weapon could not have been hidden in the smaller drawers, I took a peek anyway, examining every nook and cranny. I found paper clips in one small drawer. The next contained a roll of stamps. A third drawer, the biggest of the three, held an open box of latex gloves.

Unusual place for latex gloves.

I lifted the box and saw a hard-covered book beneath. Setting the box down on the desk, I took the book out of the drawer. My adrenalin started pumping when I read the title: *Gregg Shorthand Dictionary Simplified*, copyrighted in 1949 by the Gregg Publishing Company. Eagerly, I flipped through the well-worn book, my pulse quickening as I turned the pages and saw specific words underlined.

Bingo!

Granted, we were there solely to search for the Welrod, but this new find had all my cylinders firing. I put the book and box of gloves back exactly where I had found them and closed the drawer.

If I'd had any doubts before, finding these items were enough to make me feel certain Miss Gil had murdered Felix Romero and possibly Jessica Mont.

I strode over to the window and yanked down a single slat of the blinds. *Well I'll be damned!*

Turning my head a little to the right, I could see Mr. Romero's house, not 250 feet away.

Son of a bitch!

Elation coursing through my entire body, I turned away from the window and tore through the rest of the room, even getting on my hands and knees to check under the bed. No luck.

I took one last look around before turning off the light, closing the door and heading toward the other two bedrooms. These rooms had been painted a flat white color. The only furniture in both the rooms was a twin-sized bed, a small dresser, and a bedside table. The linoleum floors were bare, dressers and closets empty.

Next move. I went outside to check if the police had made any progress in the garage.

"She give you the garage door combination without sarcasm?" I asked, noticing the numbers panel.

"Are you kidding?" said Patrolman Danes, looking up from the bin she was inspecting. "She only gave us the combo after complaining she'd have to change the passcode when we left. Said she didn't trust us not to come back and steal her car." We both laughed.

"Find anything incriminating?"

"Nothing so far."

"Okay, thanks."

I looked around. A shovel and rake hung on one of the garage walls. On the opposite side was a wheel barrel pushed up against the wall, haphazardly piled with garden tools, a bag of fertilizer, watering cans, and garden gloves. Propped against the wall, was a forty-pound bag of potting soil, some of which had spilled onto the floor. Nothing out of the ordinary.

The worktable was bare except for three plants in small terracotta pots, kept warm by plant lights with swiveled arms bolted to the wall.

She likes plants but keeps them in the garage?

I gingerly felt the soil in one of the pots. They were all dry, although the plants looked healthy enough.

"Anybody know what kind of plants these are?"

Officer Johnson walked over for a look, picking up one of the pots and studying the plant for a few seconds. "They're probably some sort of cacti, Sir. My girlfriend has one that looks like this one."

"Thank you."

"No problem." He put down the plant and went back to his search.

I bent down and peeked inside the bag of soil.

"Anybody dig through this bag yet?" I asked.

"Yes, Sir," answered Patrolman Johnson. "Nothing in there but soil and a plastic scoop."

"I shoulda known," I said, straightening up. "Just checking."

"Way ahead of you, Sir," said the officer with a slight smile.

I nodded, also smiling.

To the right of the plant display hung a well-used ten-speed bike, anchored on wall hooks.

A cyclist. That would explain her toned physique.

I focused my attention on the shelves mounted on the wall above the wheelbarrow. There were boxes of screws, a toolbox half-filled with various kinds of screwdrivers, a hammer, several small boxes of nails, and little bins with bolts, washers, and all sorts of miscellaneous hardware. On another shelf she had what looked like an old bicycle pump and a bike chain. There was also a can full of zip ties and a roll of duct tape.

None of these items were unusual to find in a garage, but finding duct tape and plastic ties at the same residence as latex gloves, as well as a shorthand dictionary, certainly solidified the case for me against Miss Gil.

I headed back into the house where two more officers were busy emptying the kitchen drawers and cupboards. Leaving them to their task, I headed to the living room to check on our suspect. She was still working on her puzzle, pretending to be oblivious to our intrusion. I doubted we would find the murder weapon in the house today—she seemed too calm.

Detective Leung came upstairs. "Howard, come see what I found in the basement," he announced, doing nothing to modulate his voice.

From the corner of my eye, I caught Miss Gil stop moving her pencil. I could have sworn she smiled ever so slightly.

What's that about?

I followed Leung into the basement where he showed me a table piled with *Guns and Ammo, Firearms News, Handguns,* and *Rifle Shooter* magazines, with a rifle laying on top of it all.

"That's a Remington Bolt Action Rifle, Model 34, Sarge," said Leung, clearly excited.

"Is that right?"

"It's a bolt-action gun with an internal magazine, made between 1935 and 1939. Ain't she a beauty?"

"Yes, very nice," I replied. "Looks like she likes to collect old weapons."

"Not only old weapons, but bolt-action guns."

"Any sign of the Welrod?"

"Nope. No Welrod pistol down here."

I picked up the rifle to examine it more closely. Squeaky clean. I took a sniff. It looked and smelled like it hadn't been fired in a while. "Find any ammunition?" I asked.

"Not one bullet. Strange, huh?"

"Very."

"Anything in the attic?"

He checked his notebook. "An empty set of luggage, an old army trunk full of women's clothes, some shoe boxes filled with high heel shoes, a clothes rack with some really sexy dresses in zippered plastic covers, boxes of old records, some rickety old tables and lamps, and some cartons of vintage Christmas decorations."

"Find anything useful to us?"

"Nah, other than the items I mentioned, nothing more than dust, and a musty smell," he laughed.

We'd spent a couple of hours searching the property but came up empty.

The officers in the kitchen had finished their search and were quietly talking amongst themselves.

"Pack it in, guys," I ordered. "We're done here. And please tell the others in the garage."

"Yes, Sir," responded Patrolman Kent. He immediately headed out the front door, the rest of his team behind him.

I glanced at my watch. It was time to say my temporary goodbyes.

"We're leaving now, Miss Gil," I announced. She was still working her puzzle as calm as if she were relaxing on a Sunday afternoon. "Thank you for your cooperation."

Lifting her head from her magazine, she looked straight at me and asked, "Detective, what's a ten-letter word for tracker?

Oh never mind. I got it," she said before I had the chance to reply.

"B-l-o-o-d-h-o-u-n-d."

She lifted her head and smiled, her eyes cold and depthless.

Relish the moment while you can, lady. I'm coming for you.

"Good day, Ma'am," I said.

As soon as we stepped outside, and closed the door behind us, we heard a loud click of the bolt sliding into place.

We had our killer, gun, or no gun. The investigation we had worked so hard for so long had finally entered a new phase. All we had to do now was prove Miss Lillian Gil had murdered Felix Romero.

27

VOICES

She sprang from her chair as if on fire, dropping the pencil and puzzle book. Heart racing, she hastened to lock the door, leaning against it until the patrol cars drove away.

She didn't feel like dancing this time, as she had after the last time she'd watched the bloodhound sniffing around her neighborhood. This time, her heart pounded in her chest, and beads of sweat littered her forehead. To keep from freaking out and giving the *voice* an opening, she closed her eyes, placed a hand over her heart, and took slow, deep breaths. They hadn't found what they came for. They left empty handed.

A few more deep breaths brought her heartbeat back to its normal rhythm, but her mind was still racing.

How had they found her? That detective had only seen her for a second that day at the bakery. That didn't prove anything. It had to have been something else. But what? And how did they know about my treasure? That bloodhound is crafty, she had to admit.

It didn't matter. They would never find her treasure. Yet, even though they hadn't found what they came for, Anna once again felt her life was falling apart.

She slowly unlocked the door, opening it just wide enough to peek outside. When she was satisfied the cops hadn't left anyone behind, she dashed out to the garage, neglecting to grab a coat. Too anxious to feel the cold, she entered the combination and waited impatiently, tapping her foot. As soon as it opened wide enough for her to duct underneath, she scooted inside and around her car, almost colliding with the garage pole.

Her items were still hidden, still safe.

She emerged feeling less anxious, punching in the combination once again and running back to the house before the door had fully closed.

Back in the living room, Anna slumped onto the sofa. She began to shiver as her body reacclimated to the warmth of the room, and she realized how close a call that had been. She rubbed her hands and drew her knees up towards her chest. Trembling, she wrapped her arms around her shins and began to rock back and forth gnawing on her bottom lip.

He's out to get me.

The search of her property had disturbed her far more than she cared to admit.

Anna's temples began to throb. She closed her eyes and massaged her forehead. A string of conflicting emotions filled her mind. The waves of fear, anger, and hatred, unwittingly summoned an old and familiar companion.

No. Not now.

For most of her life, the *voice* in her head had made itself known whenever Anna was particularly frightened or angry. Right on schedule, the *voice* chimed in.

You stupid, pathetic girl. Did you really think you could outsmart the bloodhound?

Anna didn't feel like putting up with the *voice*. She straightened her legs and moved her hands to cover her ears, but the *voice* continued to mock her, repeating over and over—*you're going to jail, you're going to jail, you're going to jail.*

"No, no, no," she protested, violently shaking her head from side to side. "They didn't find anything."

Are you sure? the *voice* pressed.

"Not listening."

Anna bent down and reached for the puzzle book and pencil on the floor. Straightening up again, she turned to a new puzzle and tried to distract herself by reading the clues out loud, as frustrated tears rolled down her face.

Anna had come up with strategies to quiet the *voice* over the years, but in her current state of fear and agitation, she was finding it difficult.

Moments ticked by and the *voice* finally quieted, but it had already done its job. Slowly, lest it rise up again, Anna closed the book and placed it on the table with the pencil beside it.

Before she could think about it, she leaped off the sofa, ran to the basement door and yanked it open. She took the steps down two at a time, fueled by adrenaline, not even bothering to close the door behind her or switch on the overhead light. She was panting by the time she reached the bottom, not from physical exertion, but by the looming fear the *voice* might be right, and she would soon be in jail.

More frightened than she had been in years, Anna paced back and forth across the entire length of the floor, struggling to quell her anxiety. "Get a hold of yourself," she chanted over and over.

It took a while for the darkness to soothe her.

"Damn you, Felix!" she cursed out loud.

She finally pulled the chain to turn on the lamp. The forty-watt bulb gave off a dim glow, hardly penetrating the dark. Momentarily entranced by the light, she picked up the rickety old lamp and wrapped her hands around its long neck, swaying from side to side. She felt soothed by the shadowy specters the bouncing glow created on the walls and along the concrete floor.

Back in her safe space, Anna seemed to have regained her

composure, when a painful recollection surfaced from deep within her memory.

Why did you hate me, Mommy? It was a question Anna thought she'd stopped asking herself a long time ago.

She shook her head in defiance, trying to drive out the thought.

"I will not think of you," she cried out.

The auditory hallucinations had begun when she was seven years old, triggered by a beating from her mother for forgetting to fold the laundry.

If you don't cry or beg, she will leave you alone. Anna thought she had spoken the words out loud.

The next time her mother hit her, she again heard the voice. *Don't cry, don't cry.* Although all she wanted to do was scream and beg her mother to stop hitting her, she steeled herself, shut her eyes, and put her hand over her mouth so she wouldn't scream.

This puzzled her abusive mother who stopped beating her daughter, and instead began to lock her in the basement the next time she felt the urge to punish her daughter.

Alone and afraid in her mother's cold basement, the young girl made friends with the phantoms she created with an old beat-up lamp while dancing to the music in her head. The flickers of light in the semi-darkness, brought the young girl a sense of security.

Seemed like a million years ago now, when her mother had walked into the bedroom one morning carrying a box. "Here, I bought you a present," she announced. "Wake up."

The lonely girl sat up rubbing the sleep out of her eyes. She stared from her mother to the unexpected gift.

"Take it," said her mother wearing an unfamiliar smile. "It's all right," she said, shoving the box into her daughter's uncertain hands.

Unaccustomed to tenderness, the child tentatively undid the ribbon and removed the lid. Nestled in white tissue paper inside the box lay a doll made of cloth, dressed in a cotton red dress. She had long, red braids tied with red ribbons. Her beautiful face, with big, round eyes, and a wide smile, looked as if the doll was staring at her with love. Anna gasped. Her eyes had never seen such beauty. "Thank you, Mommy," she said, her little heart bursting with joy, but when she looked up, her mother had already left the room.

The doll soon became her security blanket, something tangible to hold onto during the long hours she spent trapped in that dank and dark basement.

The gift had been the only act of kindness her mother had ever shown the young girl. Two years later, mommy dearest was dead.

Good riddance, Anna thought to herself.

Weeks after the funeral, ten-year-old Anna, who was living in a group home, while Child Protective Services found a permanent home for her, was carted off to live with a distant relative whom she was told was her great aunt.

"Don't know what I ever did to deserve this, but the burden falls on me to take you in," her aunt complained, the moment the child stepped into her new home. The intimidating woman bent down until she was face to face with the frightened child, pressing her long, bony finger against her chest. "No one else wants you, so you'd better behave. By the way, from now on, your last name is Mont. Is that clear?"

"Why?" Anna asked through trembling lips, holding tightly to her doll as tears trickled down her anguished face.

"Because I don't want anyone to associate you with your crazy, whore of a mother," snapped her aunt. "I'm doing you a favor, so stop sniveling and follow me to your room so you can unpack. There are chores to be done."

As she had gotten older, Anna had begun to realize the *voice* talking in her head wasn't normal. She had learned to ignore it most of the time, but in tense moments, it overpowered her senses, leaving her vulnerable and unable to silence it. The *voice* never spoke when she was happy. She hardly heard it at all during the two years she'd spent with Felix. After he left her, the *voice* returned, mirroring her intense anger and feelings of abandonment.

The adult Anna was sitting in a pool of sweat by the time she managed to claw her way out of her trance. "Enough!" she roared. "I will not let that bloodhound get the best of me."

Feeling somewhat calmer, Anna sat at the table and tried not to dwell on the police. Soon, she began to miss her doll.

Just as she was about to drag herself upstairs, a familiar melody began to play in her mind.

Wasn't that the song you were humming when you met him? teased the *voice*.

"Shut up," Anna groaned, trying her hardest to block out the tune, until she couldn't help but think of him.

The first time they met was at a nightclub. She was Anna Mont back then, not Lillian Gil.

That evening she was sitting alone at the bar, sipping her Tom Collins, and humming along to the tune on the jukebox—Jackie DeShannon's *Bette Davis Eyes*. Felix, stylishly attired in his three-piece pin-striped suit, spotted her, and took the stool next to hers. In his most seductive tone, he declared, "This song is about you. You have those same kind of eyes."

Anna cocked her head a little and side-eyed him. She was met with a beguiling smile. When he held out his hand and asked her to dance, she was powerless to resist. When the song ended, Felix ran his fingers through her long red hair. "Your hair is so beautiful," he said, pulling her in for a kiss. She didn't resist.

They drank and danced, and made wild, passionate love that very evening. Affection-starved for so much of her life, Anna couldn't help but fall hard for him. For Felix, she brought excitement into his life again. He was the happiest he'd been since before his kids were born.

Two years later, she was waiting for him in the living room, wondering what was keeping him, when she heard the key in the lock and the doorknob turn. She rose from the sofa intending to greet him with a kiss but stopped short when the door flung open. Clearly agitated, Felix stormed in with a folded piece of paper clenched in his fist. He barely noticed the dinner she had ordered from a local restaurant, now ice cold on the table.

"Look at this," he ordered, thrusting it into her hands.

"What is it?" she asked, surprised and a little hurt by his outburst.

"Go ahead and open it," he said, his gaze cold and hard.

Her hands trembled slightly as she unfolded the paper to reveal a family tree.

"Whose family is this?" she asked, her eyes wide with confusion.

"Just look at it, will you? Look at the column on the right side of the paper."

"Okay, okay." Her eyes skimmed down the column he had pointed out. A twinge snapped in her gut when she saw the familiar name. Although she understood the implication, she chose to ignore it.

"What's this got to do with anything?" she asked, looking up from the paper as if she didn't understand.

"What's this got to do with anything?" he repeated, his tone incredulous. "Are you that stupid? We can't be together anymore. That's what this has to do with," he shouted.

Anna was frightened. The veins on the side of his forehead were popping. Panicking, she grabbed him by the arm, and tried to reason with him. "Where did you get this, anyway? Someone must be trying to trick you."

Felix yanked his arm away from her. "Nobody is trying to trick me. I did this, goddamn it." He punched the nearest wall.

Anna jumped, shocked by his outburst.

He shook his hand, knuckles red and pulsing, before explaining in a more conciliatory tone, "I spent the day going through the contents in my father's safe and piecing together what he confessed to me and my mother before he died this morning."

Anna's world was crumbling around her, and she couldn't do a thing to stop it. "Oh, I'm sorry," she mumbled.

"I know this is a shock. It is for me too, but I need you to understand," he explained in a softer tone. "Let's sit, and I'll tell you the secret my father had been hiding all these years." He took her by the hand and led her to the sofa, his expression sad and weary.

"In 1947, my father, Alberto, had an affair with a woman named Chloe Thomson," he began once they were seated.

"What's that got to do with us?" Anna asked impatiently.

"I'm getting to that."

"She bore him a daughter, born July 19, 1948. They named the baby Anna. My father did not admit paternity, so the child's name was recorded as Anna Thomson." He paused for a moment to let that sink in.

Anna made no response. She had already stopped listening. She was thinking instead of the day she had discovered her treasure, along with a stack of letters to and from Alberto Romero and Jessica Mont. In the letters, Alberto explained he was the husband of her niece, Hannah, and begged her to take in his illegitimate daughter. There was no one else related to the girl and he thought Mont would be a better caregiver than a stranger from a foster-care family. He further explained he was married with a son and could not upset his family with the news he had fathered a child outside his marriage.

"Did you hear what I said?" prompted Felix.

Anna blinked and meekly said, "My name is not Anna Thomson."

Felix's heart was breaking. He tried again to convince her. "I believed my father, but more importantly, there was plenty of evidence in that safe—letters, Anna's birth certificate, and her official adoption and name change papers. All this evidence had been locked away in my father's safe never to be acknowledged." He shook his head sadly, his eyes moist.

"None of that is true, Felix. That girl is not me."

"It is true. Let me finish."

"When Jessica declined to take in my father's daughter," Felix continued, "Alberto offered her money. After her mother's death, letters went back and forth for weeks while Anna was placed in a group home. Finally, a deal was struck, and the girl was sent to live with her great aunt, Jessica Mont, who was also my great aunt on my mother's side." A tear ran down Felix's face. "We're brother and sister, Anna."

"This can't be right, Felix," she whimpered, seizing him by the arm. "They found out about us somehow and concocted this story to break us up. I bet your mousy little wife told them about us."

Felix slapped Anna's hand away and grabbed her by the shoulders. "Did you honestly think I wouldn't check the documents carefully?" he snarled, leaning in close to her face. "You're not listening to me."

"So what?" she cried, pulling herself free of his grasp. "We love each other. Who cares what your father told you or what those papers say?"

"So what?" asked Felix, his face gradually reddening as his voice increased in volume. "I can't even believe you just said that. What kind of a person are you?" he said, looking at her in disgust, as he leapt off the sofa.

"It's over between us. You hear me?" he shouted. He didn't wait for her to respond, but rushed out of the apartment, slamming the door behind him.

Anna stared at the door, her narrowed eyes filling with rage. She scrunched the offensive paper in her hand, and then ripped it into little pieces. She stomped into the small dining area where, one by one, she smashed all the dishes, the glasses, and the wine bottle, flinging the dinner and dessert against the wall.

Feel better now? The *voice* had returned.

Anna called Felix numerous times in the days that followed, but whenever he picked up and heard her voice, he hung up immediately. Desperate, she showed up at his office, but Felix had warned security not to send her up. He even filed a restraining order against her and refused to open the door when she showed up at his home, explaining to his wife she was a crazy woman he had fired. He called the police and had her arrested. Periodically, Anna called Felix's office number to no avail. The next month, Felix stopped paying her rent. He wanted nothing to do with her. In retaliation, she mailed a stack of photos to Felix's wife.

Anna couldn't bear living without the love of her life. To keep from being evicted, she took a job at a supermarket bakery working long hours. Five years later, still mourning her lost love, she moved to Pennsylvania and began using the name Lillian Gil.

The night of the breakup had been the last time she ever saw Felix, that is, until he purchased a home right across the street from her.

To her, it felt like poetic justice. The bastard treated her like a criminal, but in the end, she exacted her pound of flesh.

He was horrified, you stupid woman, said the *voice*, making a home in her head once again.

Felix was the only person who had ever loved her. When he walked out of her life, Anna felt betrayed.

Alone in her basement in the Poconos, she let the rising anger take over. She straightened her back, pushed the chair away, and rose.

"You were wrong to leave me, Felix," she yelled into the darkness. "You were no better than my mother or that old bitch of an aunt. Fuck you all."

She clicked off the lamp and calmly walked upstairs to finish her crossword puzzle, the ghosts of her past quiet, at least for the moment.

28

ELENA'S GIFT

"She's our killer, Jun. Felt it in my bones, even before I found the evidence."

"What evidence?" Leung asked, dropping into the seat beside me, car key in hand.

"I found something while I was checking out her creepy-red bedroom."

Leung did a double take.

"Red?"

"Oh yeah. Dark red walls."

"Creepy." He shuddered.

"Very. Anyway, I was looking around in there and an old secretary desk caught my eye. I pulled out a few of the small drawers and found pens, paper clips, stamps, stationary—normal stuff people stow in a desk."

Leung inserted the key in the ignition and paused, glancing at me with one eyebrow raised. "Why do I get the feeling you hit pay dirt?"

"You could say that" I answered, a broad smile spreading across my face.

Detective Leung started the car but left it in park. He turned to face me. "Well? Don't keep me in suspense."

"There was a box of latex gloves in the bigger drawer. That in itself was enough to whet my curiosity."

"Makes sense. No fingerprints at the scene," interrupted Leung.

"The item tucked underneath the gloves is what strengthens our case even more, partner."

"Come on, Howard, out with it. What earth-shattering evidence did you find lurking beneath that box?" he blurted, impatient.

"An old *Gregg Simplified* dictionary, with shorthand symbols underlined throughout in red ink."

Leung let out a long whistle.

"And that's not all. She has a notebook on top of the desk also written in shorthand. Looks like a diary of some kind. Some of the pages are dated."

"Wow. What a find!"

"Exactly. We could arrest her now with what we have, but I'd rather wait a little longer and see what else we can dig up on her. Plus, we still have to connect her to Felix Romero. I don't want some smartass lawyer getting her off on a technicality. We need something that'll stick."

"The murder weapon," Leung offered.

"Yes. If we're correct in assuming the weapon is an old family heirloom, she must still have it stashed somewhere close."

"Detective Leung reached for the seatbelt and strapped it across his chest. "Buckle up, Sarge," he said, glancing in my direction.

I did as I was told.

"Don't you worry. Miss Lillian Gil is definitely our gal. We'll get her," he assured me as we backed out of the driveway.

When we got back to the station, the first thing I did was take out the Romero file and pull out the makeshift family tree. Not bothering to sit, I unfolded the spreadsheet and bent over my desk to study it, hoping a clue would jump out at me to connect Felix Romero and my suspect.

Felix Romero's father, Alberto Romero, had been married to Hannah Jankoski, daughter of Alexander Jankowski and Lillian Gil. They had one child, Felix. The present Lillian Gil with the same first and maiden name as Hannah's mother was too much of a coincidence to ignore. There had to be a connection, but what was it?

Frustrated, I wheeled my chair out from underneath my desk and collapsed into it. For what seemed like the hundredth time, I went over the births, marriages, and deaths of the Romero clan. Pounding my thumb repeatedly on my desk, I earnestly tried to fit the present Lillian Gil into the family tree.

This is incomplete.

There had to be a family member or members who could tie the suspect to Felix Romero.

Perhaps Mrs. Elena Romero can fill in the missing links.

I leafed through the case file until I found her number. She answered on the first ring.

"Hello, Mrs. Romero?"

"Yes, this is she."

"This is Detective Pierce."

"Who?"

"The lead detective on your husband's homicide case. You were kind enough to speak with me on the morning of the tragedy."

"Oh yes. How can I help you?" I heard the sadness in her voice and hated reminding her of that day. "I'd like to know if it's convenient for me to drop by this afternoon. There's something I need your help with."

"My help?"

"Yes, Ma'am. It won't take long."

"All right," she said. "You can come by whenever you want. I don't have anywhere to go."

"Thank you. I can be there in about twenty minutes. Is that all right?" I asked.

"That's fine, Detective. I'll start the coffee."

"Please, don't trouble yourself."

"It's no trouble, Detective."

"All right, thank you. See you soon."

"Goodbye."

I grabbed the spreadsheet and folded it before shoving it in my jacket pocket. "Kyle, please take over," I called to Hanley on my way out. "I'll be back soon."

I was already out the door when his "Aye, Sir" reached me.

———

WHEN MRS. ROMERO answered the doorbell, I almost regretted having to intrude. It took all I had not to look away when she looked in my eyes. I'd seen that same grief-stricken look in the eyes of other people who had lost loved ones in a violent manner. It's the kind of look you don't easily forget.

"Mrs. Romero. It's kind of you to see me," I said, hoping my face hadn't given away what I was thinking.

The many months that had passed since her husband's brutal murder hadn't dampened the shock of finding her husband dead in a pool of blood. If anything, she looked even more fragile now, than she had on the morning of the murder. There were dark circles beneath her eyes, and she had lost enough weight, that her dress now hung loosely from her diminished frame. She'd aged considerably since the last time I saw her.

"Please, come in. I just brewed a fresh pot of coffee. Would you like some?"

"That sounds wonderful. Thank you," I said, although I didn't really want any, but I didn't want to offend her.

Once we were settled in the living room, coffee cups on the

table between us, I took the spreadsheet out of my jacket pocket and unfolded it.

"May I?"

She nodded.

I spread the paper on the table, and smoothed out the folds, careful not to jostle the cups. Mrs. Romero watched, her eyes darting back and forth from the spreadsheet and me.

"This is a rough draft of your husband's family tree. Please take a look and see if you can help me fill in any blanks."

She picked up the makeshift Romero family tree and studied it in silence for a minute or two. "How did you get this?" she finally asked.

"My team put it together. Is there anything there you see that might be incorrect or missing?"

"You found out who Felix's maternal grandparents, and his aunt and uncle were?" she marveled. "Felix never mentioned them."

"Why did you need to know who Felix's relatives were?" she asked, tearing her eyes away from the paper.

I didn't want to admit to the grieving widow we believed the murder weapon was an antique a relative had brought back from the war.

"Sometimes looking into family members can lead us to others who can help in our investigation," I answered vaguely.

Mrs. Romero shot me a quizzical look, obviously skeptical of my explanation.

Smart woman.

She again studied the information, clearly fascinated to see her husband's lineage. I watched her carefully, my eyes glued to her face. Her eyes stopped on a particular name.

"Do you see someone you recognize?" I prompted.

"I was...I just thought when I saw Felix's parents here..."

I held my breath.

"It's just Felix once told me his father had an affair when he was eight or nine."

Father and son both had extra-marital affairs? My pulse quickened.

"Can you recall anything else he told you about the affair?"

She pulled the spreadsheet onto her lap to take a closer look. Something about this information bothered her. I remained still, barely able to hide my impatience as she pursed her lips and stared into space for what felt like an eternity.

"Let's see...Felix told me the woman was Irish, or was she Scottish? Yes, that's it, Scottish but without an accent. Probably born here in America, he thought."

"Did he happen to mention this person by name?"

"Oh my. This was so long ago," she said, her brow furrowed.

"Take your time," I encouraged. "Anything you can recall, no matter how trivial, will be of great help." She slowly shook her head, chewing her lip.

"Wait a minute. I found an envelope when I was going through Felix's things after..." She swallowed, and quickly composed herself. "I think there's something in there that may be of help to you. I'm sorry I didn't think of it right away."

"No need to apologize," I said, anxious to get my hands on that envelope.

She ran her fingers through her now shoulder-length, almost completely white hair. I noticed she still wore her wedding ring.

"Honestly, I don't know where my mind is these days."

She set the spreadsheet on the table and hurried away. Quite a few minutes went by, giving me more than enough time to finish my now, lukewarm coffee.

I was starting to think she wasn't coming back when she rushed into the living room holding a large, manila envelope. "Sorry that took so long. I'd forgotten what box I put this in."

"Not at all. I was enjoying the coffee," I lied.

Mrs. Romero smiled, and there, standing before me was the beautiful woman she had once been.

She sat and moved the spreadsheet onto her lap again.

"Felix saved some family pictures and letters," she said, handing me the envelope.

"Thank you."

I undid the fastener, reached in, and pulled out a few photographs, a couple of letters, and a four by four-inch envelope. I studied the postmarks on the letters and noticed they'd both been mailed from New York in the 1970s, only a couple of weeks apart.

"Mrs. Romero, do you happen to know who wrote these letters?"

"Yes," she whispered, staring down at her lap.

Something about them was obviously making her uncomfortable.

"Would you mind telling me who wrote them?"

Posture slumping ever so slightly, she drew in a long, deep breath through her nose and blew it out her mouth. "They were written by Felix's mistress," she divulged with barely concealed venom.

Her husband kept old love letters from his mistress? Why hadn't Mrs. Romero destroyed them?

I was anxious to read the letters, but of course, I couldn't do so in front of the widow. I changed the subject.

"Can you tell me who the people in the photographs are?"

Mrs. Romero reached for the pile, shuffling through them, and pulling one out. "I don't know most of these people. In particular, I have no idea who that baby is. Felix was an only child and as far as he knew, he didn't have any cousins."

I stared at the black and white photo, trying to commit every detail and nuance to memory. On the other side, it was date stamped July 22, 1948.

"Is there anyone you do recognize?"

She sifted through the pictures, passing me each one she found where she recognized someone. "These are Felix's parents, both deceased. This one is Felix when he was a teen, this one is Felix with his mother, and this is his grandmother on his mother's side," she told me.

I saw an inscription, now faded, on the back of the picture. *From Lillian with love.*

I could see the family resemblance in most of the pictures she had shown me thus far.

Mrs. Romero pulled out another photo and stared at it for a moment before she said, "This is a picture of my husband's mistress."

Her voice cracked and her hand shook slightly as she passed over this last photograph.

In the photo, a smiling young woman sat on a park bench, her long legs crossed. It was the only one in color, and the only one not date stamped. My heart skipped a beat when I took in her magnificent red hair, highlighted by the pale summer dress she was wearing. Her beautiful eyes held my gaze. I'd seen those eyes before.

Not wanting to add to Mrs. Romero's distress, I thanked her and turned the photo over, placing it face down on the table.

She leaned forward and arranged the rest of the pictures into a neat pile.

One particular photo on top of the pile caught my attention. A man and a woman, standing close together in an office, his arm around her waist. They were laughing. I picked it up and showed it to Mrs. Romero. "Do you know who these people are?"

"Oh, yes. Sorry, didn't mean to skip that one. That's Alberto, Felix's dad. I have no idea who the woman is, probably a co-worker."

This was getting more and more fascinating by the minute.

I placed it back on the stack and picked up the small envelope. Inside was a torn piece of notebook paper with the names Chloe Thomson and Anna Thomson written in pencil.

"Did Felix ever mention the names Chloe Thomson or

Anna Thomson?" I asked.

She creased her eyebrows. "I've never heard of them. Maybe they're also relatives?"

"Yes, probably," I agreed.

I focused my attention on a piece of microfiche tucked in the small envelope. Holding it up to the light, I could just make out what appeared to be a birth certificate.

This was important. Felix wouldn't have saved it otherwise.

Mrs. Romero watched me intently but didn't say anything further.

"Mind if I take these items with me, Mrs. Romero?"

"No, of course not, but I really don't understand how knowing Felix's family history will help you."

"In my experience, small things often turn out to be big clues in an investigation."

"Well, you're the expert," she shrugged.

I gathered up the items, slid them back into the manila envelope, ready to leave. Mrs. Romero gave the spreadsheet back to me.

I had to know. "Mrs. Romero, I hope you don't think me impertinent, but if the letters are from your husband's mistress..." I trailed off.

"I know what you're going to say to me. Why didn't I tear them up?"

"Yes, Ma'am."

"I haven't been able to bring myself to read those letters yet, Detective. And yes, part of me wants to rip them up and throw them in the fire, but I held onto them because I do want to read them eventually. I would rather know the truth, no matter how awful. I guess I feel like I need to know if this was just a fling, or if Felix really loved that woman," she confessed with a sad smile.

"I understand." I didn't really, but I was grateful she hadn't destroyed them.

"I'll get these back to you as soon as the investigation is

over."

"No hurry, Detective."

"Thank you again, Mrs. Romero."

She squeezed my hand. There was no mistaking the pain in her eyes when she pleaded, "Please catch Felix's killer."

"I will, Mrs. Romero. You can count on it."

———

When I entered the squad room, I was met with what looked like a weeks' worth of empty coffee cups and over-flowing wastebaskets. It was plain to see the frustration etched across the faces of my crew.

"Gather around people," I commanded.

When I had everyone's attention focused on me, I filled them in on the treasure trove Mrs. Romero had provided.

"Yes! The end is near," said O'Malley, pumping a fist in the air. The whole group cheered, smacking each other on the back, and hi-fiving. I patiently waited for the end of their cele-bration.

"Kyle, would you please take this microfiche over to the library," I requested once the cheering had subsided. "Make a copy of whatever is on that film and bring it back to me as soon as you can, please."

Hanley reached for the envelope. "Will do, Sarge."

"Ceci, we need to know if Anna Mont legally changed her name to Lillian Gil. I've got a feeling she may not be who she says she is. Also, see if you can find a birth certificate for Anna Thomson or Anna Romero, whose mother may have been Chloe Thomson. Anna was probably born in New York State, likely around the late forties or early fifties."

"On it."

"All right, that's all for now, folks. Thank you." Before returning to my office, I decided to rib them.

"By the way, clean up around here, will you, guys? This

place is beginning to look like a pig sty."

O'Malley reacted with his usual smart-alecky remark. "Did you just call us pigs, Sarge? You know us police don't like being called pigs."

"If the trough fits," I answered, enjoying the banter.

Everyone roared with laughter.

"Good one, Sarge," Celia called out, elbowing the laughing O'Malley in the ribs.

"All right, let's get back to work," I ordered.

Just like that, the break in our case injected much needed energy into the team.

I returned to my desk and reached for my rolodex. When I found the card, I dialed Detective Jones.

"Hello, Howard. Solve the case already?" he answered with a hearty laugh.

"Not yet, Fred, but soon."

"Excellent. How may I assist you?"

"I was wondering if you had come across someone named Anna Thomson, or Chloe Thomson when you were investigating the Jessica Mont homicide?"

"That's T-h-o-m-s-o-n, and Anna with one or two n's?"

"Yes, and Anna with two n's."

"Those names don't sound familiar, but I'll get right on it and call you back soon as I can."

"Thanks, pal."

"No problem. Feels good to be detecting again." I yanked the receiver away from my ear as he roared his mighty laugh into the phone.

"Talk to you soon, Fred."

"Bye, Howard."

I allowed myself a short moment to reflect, after hanging up. There was no denying Mrs. Romero had given our case a much-needed boost. However, I had a strong gut feeling it was Felix himself who may have solved his own murder. The end to this nightmare of a case was well within my reach.

29

LIGHTNING BOLT

The suspect was under constant surveillance after the failed search of her property. We watched as she biked, jogged, bought groceries, and went to and from work at the bakery, never deviating from her daily routine. Perhaps she knew we were watching.

It became more and more apparent with each passing day, she wasn't about to make a wrong move, now that she knew we were on to her. Nothing worse than a stalled case when we were this close to the finish line.

Yawning, I stretched and reached for my third cup of luke-warm coffee. I didn't normally indulge this much anymore, Louise having long ago weaned me off of my nine to ten cups a day habit. Today though, I needed the added energy. I had been up most of the night surveilling Miss Gil's residence. *This better be my last cup today or I'll regret it.*

Going through the paperwork gathered over many months of this investigation, there was enough evidence to take her into custody. We couldn't continue surveillance on the depart-ment's dime much longer, in the off chance she would lead us to the weapon.

Detective Byrne managed to get her hands on a copy of the

name change application filed by Miss Jessica Mont on behalf of her niece, Anna Thomson, approved back in 1958 when Anna first went to live with her great aunt.

"I couldn't find any documentation for a name change from Anna Mont to Lillian Gil," Byrne reported. "As far as I can determine, Anna Mont began using the name, *Lillian Gil* when she moved to Pennsylvania."

"Check with Social Security for me, will you? She might be working with a bogus number. If that's the case, she'll be going down for fraud too."

"Or she could be getting paid under the table and not filing taxes, in which case her boss would also need to be investigated for tax evasion."

"Good point. Look into that and let me know what you find, please. Anything on her parents, by the way?"

"Yes, Sir." She reached into a file folder and pulled out a *New York State Certificate of Death.*

"This is Chloe Thomson's death certificate," she said, handing me the paper.

The details did not surprise me. Female, Caucasian, Age 36. Date of death: August 21, 1958, Cause of death: Suicide by Exsanguination. Coincides with the year Anna went to live with her aunt at age ten.

I passed the death certificate back to Celia. "What else have you got for me?"

"I called and interviewed the director of Robertson's Funeral Home in Manhattan, where Chloe Thomson's service was held."

"How did you find the funeral home where she was laid out?"

"Simple. Her last known address in Manhattan is listed on the death certificate. I just looked up funeral parlors in Manhattan until I found it."

"Impressive."

"Thanks. Anyway, the funeral director searched through his files and confirmed the suicide."

"Thank you, Detective. Great work."

She smiled.

Detective Byrne made my job so much easier.

I pondered the Romero homicide case files stacked neatly on my desk. With a strong case against Anna, I should just go ahead and make the arrest. Why was I stalling?

The murder weapon. I wanted it, pure and simple. My gut told me she wouldn't have gotten rid of it. According to Leung's friend's story, she'd called it "my treasure." Yeah, she loves that old gun.

Drumming my fingers atop the files only increased my caffeine-induced nervous energy. One last review.

I began with the letters Mrs. Romero had provided, which connected Felix Romero to his former lover, Anna. The same Anna adopted by her distant relative, Jessica Mont, shortly after her mother passed away. I read the first letter Romero received.

Please Felix, you can't throw our love away like garbage. It doesn't matter what people think. Why are you always so worried what others have to say? They don't know how deep our love is. I know you'll see I'm right once you calm down. Please come back to me. I miss you. Anna

The second letter, written a few weeks later, took a different tone.

Damn you, Felix. Do you know how embarrassing it was to be escorted out of your office building? And a restraining order, seriously? You had me arrested because I went to your house hoping we could talk? How dare you?

How could you do that to me? You won't even return my calls or answer my letters. For the last time, so what if your stupid father and my crazy mother were lovers? We're only half brother and sister. It doesn't mean anything. Why can't you forget about that? You're a coward and I'll never forgive you. Go ahead, stay with your mousy little wife who you don't even love. You don't deserve me. I know you dream about me when you lie with her. I know you do, you bastard. You'll be sorry. I hate you, you gutless little man. Anna

INTO THE EVIDENCE box went the letters. Next, I reached for the microfiche with Anna Thomson's birth certificate. Born July 19, 1948. Mother - Chloe Thomson. Father - unknown.

Elena Romero had told me about Felix's father's affair. Anna's father had to have been Alberto Romero.

I shuffled the pile of photos Mrs. Romero had given me and pulled out the black and white picture of the unknown baby, date stamped July 22, 1948. Three days after Anna was born.

Mrs. Romero had to have known the baby was the illegitimate child of Alberto Romero. No need to question her again though, she'd given us enough valuable details to help us solve her husband's murder.

I propped my elbow on my desk and held my chin, mulling over what I knew.

Felix found out Anna was his half-sister and ended the affair. Anna was furious. Years later, Felix unknowingly moved across the street from his former lover and sister, who seized the opportunity for revenge.

I drained the last of my now cold and bitter coffee.

What a world.

Despite his infidelity, not to mention his resentful and unfriendly nature, Felix Romero didn't deserve such a brutal end to his life.

As I gathered the rest of the paperwork, my eyes landed on the image of the Welrod pistol. I gnawed on my cheek, as I tried to imagine where in the house a person would hide such a weapon. I must have been contemplating for longer than I realized. The inside of my cheek was beginning to ache.

Damn it. Where in hell could she have hidden it? We'd gone through her house with a fine-toothed comb and we still hadn't found it.

I did an internet search for the firearm, hoping to find images of all its parts. It had already occurred to me more than once, she may have disassembled the gun before hiding it, but things had been moving so fast, I put off acting on my hunch.

A half hour passed, as I surfed around the internet. I read up on the history of the gun, when it was last used in war, and any other interesting facts about the Welrod I could find, but nowhere could I find images of the components that made up the pistol.

I gripped the mouse tighter with each unsatisfactory search, feeling the muscles in my hand begin to lock and ache. I clenched my teeth and felt the vein on the side of my head begin to pulse.

Exasperated, I let go of the mouse and opened and closed my fist, trying to get some circulation back. Discouraged, I closed my eyes and massaged my temples.

Damn. Better call an expert.

"Leung," I yelled. "Would you please come in here?"

"What's up, Boss?" he asked, poking his head into my office. He looked fresh as a daisy after a day off, his stylishly cut jet-black hair glistening, and his clothes neatly pressed.

"I'm trying to find a diagram of the Welrod pistol after it's been taken apart. Could you help me? I'm not having any luck."

He gave me an almost cocky grin as he walked around the desk. "Move, Sarge," he requested. "Let a professional handle this."

I got up and offered him my chair.

Leung dropped into my seat and started typing and clicking, muttering under his breath every few seconds. I hovered behind him, anxiously chewing the inside of my cheek.

The search felt like it took much longer than it did. Less than five minutes had passed, when he suddenly said, "Voila!"

He had landed on a page showing drawings of the various parts that make up the gun. I felt my body relax.

"You're a miracle worker, Detective," I said, gratefully squeezing his shoulders.

"You just have to know how to search, that's all," he answered as he got out of my chair.

"Good job, pal. Thanks," I said, patting him on the back. "Now get out of here and let me get back to work."

He marched out looking pleased, no doubt on his way to tell the others how indispensable he is to me. I heard laughter pouring through my open door a few minutes later.

The webpage displayed lots of little pieces that go inside the gun. When assembled, the Welrod is a little over fourteen inches in length with a weight of forty-two and one-half ounces.

As I stared at all the parts, the answer hit me like a bolt of lightning.

Shit, that's it! I thought, slapping my forehead.

The telephone rang just as I clicked on the print icon. I debated letting it go to voicemail but thought it might be important.

"Detective Pierce," I snapped, annoyed by the interruption.

"Hi, Howard. It's Fred."

Shit. I'd forgotten to call him.

"Oh hey, Fred. Got something for me?" I asked in a more cordial tone.

"Sorry, Howard. I couldn't find anyone named Thomson anywhere in my investigation."

I felt bad to have wasted his time. "About that…I'm the one who should apologize. I was going to call you, but things have been moving fast around here."

"What's happened?"

"We managed to get a copy of the birth certificate for Anna Mont, who was born Anna Thomson."

"Don't tell me her mother's name is Chloe Thomson."

"It is. Not only that, but Mrs. Romero was kind enough to let me examine some personal photos and correspondence, which supports the fact Anna Thomson's father is Alberto Romero, my homicide victim's father."

"Wow. That kind of luck doesn't happen too often."

"I'll say. We also learned my suspect began using the same name as the victim's maternal grandmother, Lillian Gil, when she moved to Pennsylvania."

"No!" he exclaimed.

"Anna Thomson, aka Anna Mont, aka Lillian Gil, are one and the same person."

Detective Jones belted out one of his lion roars. I moved the receiver away from my ear, but not before I felt the reverberations of his laughter. He was still guffawing as he sputtered, "Won't be long before our suspect is in handcuffs."

"We have a good strong case this time, Fred. As a matter of fact, I just got an idea for where to look for the murder weapon. If I'm right, we'll have the final piece of the puzzle."

"You don't say? That's great news, Howard. Thank you for putting the final period on that cold case of mine. Can't wait to look Miss Thomson, Mont, Gil, whatever her name is, in the face."

"Actually, it's Mont. She never bothered to change it legally when she began using the name Gil."

"Little did she know, the name Gil would lead you to connect her to both our homicide victims."

"Funny how things work out like that. And Fred, I just want to say, I couldn't have done it without your help. I mean that sincerely."

"I appreciate that, Howard, but hard work is what cracked this case wide open. Good luck today."

"Talk to you soon, Detective."

I hung up, marched over to the printer, and grabbed the schematics to the Welrod. I then typed up the affidavit, detailing all evidence gathered to justify the arrest. I picked up the phone again to request a search and arrest warrant authorization.

On my way to get Leung, Hanley grabbed me. "Got a letter for you, Sarge," he said, handing me the latest correspondence from Miss Lillian Gil. I was beginning to think she'd forgotten about me. She must be feeling safe again.

I returned to my desk and slit the envelope open. This time, the envelope contained a sheet of notebook paper, rather than the usual index card.

I scanned this latest correspondence and emailed it to Aunt Maddy.

Eager to make the arrest, I paced while I waited for Maddy's response. Ten minutes later, Aunt Maddy's email arrived. I smiled when I read the translation.

"Detective Leung, come with me, please," I called as I rushed through the squad room. "We're finally on our way to end this investigation."

Leung practically jumped out of his chair.

We picked up the warrant and headed to Birdview Lane.

I was a little worried we might have spooked Anna into moving the firearm, but weapon or no weapon, this was her last day of freedom. I had her in my sights.

Leung and I once again took our positions on either side of Mont's front door.

A back-up unit circled around to the back of the house in case she, or anyone else, fled.

Leung banged on the door.

"Wait a moment, will you?" she yelled.

Leung and I locked eyes and nodded, prepared for anything.

30

THE ARREST

Anna jumped from the sofa when she heard police sirens.

They're coming for you, the *voice* taunted.

She bolted up the stairs to her bedroom and snatched her doll off the bed. Clutching her prized possession to her chest, she pivoted, and raced all the way down to the basement.

Heart beating a mile a minute, Anna grabbed the Remington she'd previously loaded in anticipation of this moment. Taking the steps two at a time, she ran back upstairs, where the knocking had become insistent.

Kill them all.

Heart threatening to jump out of her chest, sweat clouding her eyes, hair sticking to her face, she hugged the doll tightly, while holding the rifle with a sweaty and shaky hand.

She took a deep breath in, closing her eyes and rocking back and forth as she tried to calm her fears.

Don't let them take you to jail. You won't like it there.

"*Be Quiet!*" she shrieked.

Working hard to control her breathing, she steeled herself with the same coldness she had channeled to torture her former lover. Her moment of dread passed as quickly as it had risen. Gently placing her doll on the floor, she wiped her face with the back of her hand and smoothed the hair away from her eyes.

She tiptoed toward the door, undoing the bolt, and quickly backing away. She planted her feet and aimed the rifle at the door, finger on the trigger, ready to fire at anyone coming through.

"They're not taking me to jail," she whispered, blinking the sweat out of her eyes.

Yes, they are, you stupid girl, said the *voice.*

"Shut Up!"

Leung and I exchanged looks when we heard her first shout. Could someone else be in there with her?

"This is the police," I called out. "We have a warrant for your arrest. Open the door."

We heard the click of the lock and another shout. When the door still did not open, I tried one more time.

"This is the police. We have a warrant for your arrest. Open the door."

No answer. I reached for the doorknob and signaled to Leung, who crouched low and readied his weapon.

I took a breath, reached over and slowly twisted the doorknob. With a forceful push, the door swung open.

A shot rang out.

Leung immediately reacted and returned fire.

The unit in the back of the house rammed the back door in the moment they heard the shots, charging in at the same moment as Leung and I.

"You shot me, you sons of bitches," Anna screamed from the floor, attempting to aim the rifle with shaky hands. Leung yanked the gun away from her, passed it to me so he could force her arms behind her and cuff her.

"Someone please call an ambulance," I ordered.

"Yes Sir," responded one of the officers, radioing 911.

Another officer tried to put pressure on her wound. "Don't touch me," she screamed, pushing his hand away.

"If you don't want to bleed to death, I suggest you let him apply pressure to that leg," I said.

I watched as her face changed from pain, to hate, to fury, and finally to defeat, all in a matter of seconds. If I hadn't been focused on her reaction, I would have missed the show. It was like witnessing a Jekyll and Hyde transformation.

"Anna Mont, you're under arrest for the murder of Felix Romero."

She gave me such a pitiful look, I almost felt sorry for her.

As I finished reciting the Miranda Warning, the vicious killer, finally in handcuffs, donned a crooked smile.

"Congratulations, Detective Bloodhound. You got me," she spat through labored breath.

There she is.

"That's me," I winked, "Detective Bloodhound."

"Tell me, Miss Mont, where are you hiding that treasure of yours?"

I couldn't tell which surprised her more, my discovering her pet name for the murder weapon, or my calling her by her legal name.

"Never mind. I know exactly where to find it."

I walked out the front door just as the EMTs came through.

Perhaps because of the pain she was in, the loss of blood, or the fact she no longer had any secrets to keep, Miss Mont had no more will to resist. As the EMTs prepped her for transport, she pleaded, "Give me my doll. I need my doll."

By the time EMT's had loaded her into the ambulance, calmed and clutching her doll, I had already punched in the combination to the garage door. Thankfully, she had not changed the code as she'd threatened last time we paid her a visit.

Impatient and anxious, I ducked underneath the door as

soon as it was halfway up, Leung right behind me. I headed straight for the shelf where I had last seen it and breathed a sigh of relief. It was still there. What I originally mistook for an old bicycle pump, turned out to be the suppressor, the main part of the Welrod, right there in plain sight.

Gotta hand it to her. She's shrewd.

I grabbed the silencer and brought it over to the worktable. I pushed the three flower pots to the side and pulled out the printed schematics for comparison.

Leung was admiring the part. "Impressive, isn't it?"

"Yes, Jun. Let's find the rest."

"Can't wait to see the entire weapon put together," said Jun, his eyes shining with excitement.

"Help me dig inside those boxes, will you, Jun? We're looking for these pieces," I said pointing to the schematics.

Leung barely needed to glance at the paper, such was his familiarity with firearms. Working together, we sifted through all the hardware boxes, searching for the parts in the diagram.

"Look what I found," Leung exclaimed after emptying a toolbox full of wrenches. I stopped what I was doing and stared at what he so proudly waved in my face. "This is the short magazine piece that acts as the grip for the weapon," he explained with a broad grin.

Of course, my weapons expert knew immediately what he'd found.

"I'm guessing all the parts are in here somewhere. Can't believe we missed these large pieces last time," I said.

Leung raised an eye-brow at me. I knew exactly what he was thinking. Perhaps if he'd been the one searching the garage when we were first here, instead of exploring the attic and basement, we would have found the pieces of the Welrod pistol sooner. Thankfully, Jun wasn't the kind to point fingers.

"I'll keep looking," he said without comment, laying the grip on the table with the suppressor. A few minutes later, we had found all the various washers and baffles that go inside the cylinder.

"So simple and yet so damn impressive," Leung commented after we had all the parts laid out in front of us.

"That it is, Jun. But where are the bullets? They have to be around here somewhere."

"If I were a bullet, where would I hide?" Jun jokingly asked.

"They can't be far. Probably in plain sight," I said.

Without another thought, I grabbed the flowerpots and upended them. Out poured the plants, soil, and the bullets.

Gotcha!

EPILOGUE
CHERRY ON THE CAKE

When Anna Mont was released from the hospital, Leung and I were there to escort her to the precinct.

True to form, and despite being under the influence of pain killers, she reacted like a trapped animal, fighting to free herself from Jun's strong grasp.

"Let me go. You have no right to do this," she screamed, tugging, and pulling, but she was no match for Leung. He wrestled her into the back of the cruiser in no time at all.

Defeated, she stopped struggling.

As we drove, I took a peek into the rearview mirror every once in a while to check in on our prisoner. Head shaking, she moved her shoulders up toward her ears as if trying to cover them, muttering something unintelligible. At one point she hollered, *"Be Quiet!"*

Jun and I exchanged glances. He turned toward the back-seat, and in his most intimidating tone, ordered, "Shut your mouth, will ya?"

Though she continued shaking her head and mumbling to herself, she at least stopped yelling for the rest of the ride.

Cuffing her to the bar on the table in the interrogation room, I thanked Miss Mont for making it easy to find the murder weapon.

"What weapon?" she snarled, but I could see surprise in her eyes.

I reached into my pocket and took out her latest correspondence, transcribed once again by Aunt Maddy. Relishing every second, I cleared my throat and began to read.

Dear bloodhound. You found me. Score one for you. But you left empty handed. I enjoyed watching you and your friends chasing your tails. I bet it was frustrating not to have found what you came for.

"Shall I go on?" I asked.

"Knock yourself out," she sneered.

I smiled and continued.

You can sniff around for my treasure like the dog you are. You'll never prove I killed that worthless piece of shit, but feel free to do your bloodhound act. You have nothing. Felix abandoned me. Years later, after I had made a life for myself in the Poconos, the son of a bitch decides to move here, and right across the street from me. Fate was practically begging me to kill him. I obliged, and it felt good. Karma really is a bitch.

"Thank you for your confession, but it wasn't necessary," I said, folding the note and slipping it back in my pocket. "My team of bloodhounds sniffed out all the evidence we need to put you in prison for the rest of your life."

It's jail time, the *voice* mocked.

Anna flinched and shook her head, muttering under her breath before she turned her attention back to me.

I swear I could feel the force of her pent-up rage and hate emanating from those lovely eyes of hers. I turned and walked out, leaving Leung to process her for arraignment.

———

"HELLO."

"Hi Fred, Howard here."

"Howard! Give me the good news."

"You can start the extradition paperwork for Miss Anna Mont."

"You did it, Howard, you got her."

"*We* did it, Fred," I corrected him. "You gave me the background I needed to fit all the pieces together. I know I said this before, but I really mean it. I couldn't have done it without you."

"You're too kind, but I'm sure you would have solved this one with or without my help. I'm just glad we can both finally close the books on our cases. Let me know when you have a trial date, I'd like to be there."

"I will, and when you get out here, you can stay with Louise and me. We have plenty of room for you and Sophia if she'd like to come. I'm sure Louise would love to meet her."

"Thank you. Sophie would love to meet Louise, as would I."

"See you, Fred. I'll call with that trial date soon as I have it."

"You made my day, Howard. See you soon."

———

BECAUSE OF THE preponderance of evidence against Anna Mont, her attorney didn't have much of a defense. She was found guilty of premeditated murder in the case of Felix Romero, and soon after extradited to New York City where she was again found guilty of premeditated murder in the case of Jessica Mont. The Commonwealth of Pennsylvania remanded Anna Mont, and after a psychiatric evaluation, declared her mentally ill. She is receiving care at Norristown Psychiatric Hospital where she will live out the rest of her days incarcerated, with no possibility of parole.

Anna Wagner was arrested for not paying taxes on Anna Mont's wages. She faces stiff penalties and jail time.

As for me, I retired on time. Record intact.

ACKNOWLEDGMENTS

Mistakes. We all make them. I certainly did when I jumped headfirst into the band wagon of self-publishers. Erotic fiction was popular a few years ago, so I thought, *yeah, I can write one of those*. Big mistake. The book got good reviews until it tanked, having run out of sales from family, co-workers, and friends, I suspect. I suppose it also had a lot to do with my very limited social media presence and my faith in word-of-mouth.

Because I love to write, and because I had experienced the high an author gets when holding in her hands a novel she created, I again wrote and, you guessed it, self-published another book, this time a story about child sexual abuse. Don't judge. The best lessons learned are the ones learned by making mistakes. With the harsh reality the books were not up to par, I took them off the market. I do have to thank the ladies at the Sisters Uptown Bookstore for welcoming me and my books with open arms. They actually loved the erotic book—not so much the other.

A phrase attributed alternately to Buddhism and Theosophy states: *When the Student is ready, the Teacher will Appear.* In my case, a whole group of teachers stepped into my life to help this misguided, but passionate, writer. I will forever be grateful to Katherine Hernandez for the introduction to my Lady Writers group. These accomplished writers took me by the hand and explained character development, importance of dialogue, scene description, as well as proper formatting. Because of these wonderful ladies, I am proud to call my friends, Simply Gregg is the best work I have ever written. With love and admiration, I sincerely thank Sahar R. Abdulaziz, Belinda M. Gordon, Katherine Hernandez, Kelly Jensen, Susan M. Jordan, MaryAnne Moore, Catherine Schratt, and Laurel Wilczek.

Thank you, Michael A. Ventrella for answering my legal, and non-legal questions. To my Beta readers, Maria L. Alonzo, Alvin Joaquin Figueroa Gil de Lamadrid, Michael J. Tyrell, and Paul Quillin, much appreciation for reading the raw manuscript and for your helpful comments.

Thank you, Warren Leyberry, my Developmental Editor, for your initial edits and suggestions. A big thank you to Tracy Michael, Editor. Although you made lots of comments in red, I began to see where moving things around, helped the flow of the story. The manuscript is much improved with your help.

It only took a couple of tries before the very talented Wesley Goulartt designed the perfect book cover for my story. A million thanks, Wes. I love your work.

A special thank you to Detective Richard Wolbert, who years ago when I began writing Simply Gregg, took the time to meet with me and answer my many questions. I hope you are enjoying your retirement.

Last but certainly not least, I want to thank my husband, Richard, for not only his encouragement and belief I could write a best seller (fingers crossed) but for understanding how important writing is to me. Thank you for adjusting our work schedule, freeing time for me to write.

ABOUT THE AUTHOR

Evelyn Infante is a small business owner, living in the beautiful Pocono Mountains of Pennsylvania, with her husband, Richard.

Ever since she could remember, writing has been a passion for this author. She self-published two books, which were modestly received. Realizing they were not up to par, Evelyn took them off the market to further improve her craft. Doing research for a novel about a local detective trying to solve a homicide, has opened up a new world for her. She has found a new and exciting genre to explore.

Evelyn knows writing is an everlasting learning experience. Even the most accomplished writers can always make a story better. After much research, writing and rewriting, she has finally found her groove.

facebook.com/Writing4Joy

twitter.com/EInfanteAuthor

instagram.com/evelyninfante99

Made in the USA
Monee, IL
25 April 2021

66815455R00148